VENGEANCE
BEYOND REASON

06/02

To Jane,

Thanks for the encouragment

Frani

VENGEANCE BEYOND REASON

●

Joani Ascher

AVALON BOOKS
NEW YORK

PRINTED IN THE UNITED STATES OF AMERICA
ON ACID-FREE PAPER
BY HADDON CRAFTSMEN, BLOOMSBURG, PENNSYLVANIA

This book is for my husband, David, with all my love.

I would like to thank the many people who supported my efforts to become a writer. Among others are Deborah Nolan, Jane Degnan, Mary Elizabeth Allen, Kim Zito, Fredericka Glucksman and Mark Podolsky, great writers all. I would also like to thank the South Orange, New Jersey, police department for answering my questions, my editor, Paula Decker, and my wonderful family.

Chapter One

Brian Lambert spent the last fifteen minutes of his life feeling sorry for himself.

Since he was unaware that his life was about to end, but knew that his hands were cold, he stuffed them deeper into his coat pockets. As a not-so-perfect end to a not-so-perfect day, he had left his gloves on the table in the student union where he had one last cup of hot chocolate to fortify himself for the long walk back to his room.

He had to face it. His whole college experience so far was not perfect. He had been closed out of the MWF English class, and the professor of the longer TTH class had a way of droning that left Brian pinching himself to stay awake. His calculus professor spoke little English, none of it intelligible, and he was already behind in both biology and chemistry. Finally, as if he weren't miserable enough, his college was located in Grosvenor, New Jersey.

When his mother brought him to look at the school, he discovered that from the higher elevations of the little town the spectacular skyline of New York City was visible. But as Brian walked home from school on Wednesday evening, he could not see it, any more than he could see what was coming. He was near the bottom of the hill, seeing only the dark street in front of him, and not much of that. This street, like the rest of the streets in the town, was not straight. The streets of Grosvenor looked like they had been laid out by people who were too tired or lazy to make sense out of the mountain in the Watchung chain upon which the town was built. Later developers of New Jersey made straight streets with names that sounded like they belonged together, but Grosvenor was settled long before that.

Like Lima, Ohio, which was pronounced like the bean, and Versailles, Indiana, which was pronounced Ver Sales, the people of Gross Venor, as Brian thought of it, pronounced it just as it looked. He could hardly believe he had ended up there.

Brian had taken a room in a house about two miles from the campus because it was the cheapest living arrangement he could make. The landlady didn't bother him, didn't even pay any attention to him, despite his mother's requests that the old woman keep an eye on her baby boy, her only child.

His mother had approved of the college, St. Michael's, probably because it was small and Catholic, and his acceptance letter had come with a scholarship offer. Although it broke her heart, she had actually accepted that he wasn't going to one of the big-name schools. This small private university was the best he could do after his grades dipped in his crucial junior year of high school, courtesy of the most demanding and difficult-to-please girlfriend in the world.

All this girlfriend wanted to do was become Mrs. Brian Lambert, right away, and have babies as soon as possible, even if that meant that Brian would have to give up his plans of becoming a pharmacist. As soon as he sent in his applications for college, with his spectacularly lowered credentials, she dumped him.

He shook off the painful memories as he turned onto

Brookside Lane. It was much darker there, with long shadows cast by bare, overhanging trees. Rushing water in the brook that ran beneath the bushes nearly obscured the other autumn sound of brittle leaves crunching under his feet. Inhaling deeply, he smelled their fragrance. It was mingled with that of a wood fire coming from a fireplace in one of the large, comfortable houses that lined the road. It only made him miss his home more.

A muffled cry shook him out of his reverie just as the road turned sixty degrees to the right and inclined steeply. A huge clump of bushes obscured the sidewalk ahead. The light from the gas lamps along the street was so dim that Brian could not see who made the noise, but he thought it sounded female, young, and frightened.

"Who's there?" he whispered into the dark, fear spilling into his own voice.

There was no answer, just the snap of a branch and a grunt. Brian stood paralyzed by fright.

The voice cried out, louder this time. "Let me go. I'm not . . ." was all he could make out.

"D-do you need help?" he asked in the general direction of the sound. He pushed his way into the bushes, uncertain of what he would find, unable to ignore the cries.

He had almost come out of the bushes on the other side when he felt something knife through his sweater. It pierced his flesh and twisted upward, which caused unbelievable searing pain as it severed crucial blood vessels.

As he fell, he heard a gasp from somewhere above him, more struggling, and then quiet, just before he passed out. The chilly ground did not do much to stanch the blood which was gushing out of him, taking his life, his dreams, and his mother's hopes with it.

The death of the college student missed the 6:00 news because the body was not found until nearly 8:30 by a man taking his beagle for a walk. Preferring the flatter part of

the hill, he headed down that way. His normally cooperative dog surprised him when he stopped at that annoying
clump of bushes and refused to move. The dog's plaintive
whines led to the startling discovery.

Starting at 9:00, promos ran every ten minutes or so for
the story, even before the field reporter could get her car
out to Grosvenor for the live feed.

Telephone wires buzzed. By 11:00, the news channels of
the tri-state area had the attention of nearly everyone in the
town of Grosvenor, including Wally Morris. She sat
propped up in bed in the dark next to her husband, Nate,
staring at the spot of light from their television. The tiny
nursery school teacher got goose bumps as she recognized
a street she drove along every day.

"In our lead story tonight," the meticulously groomed
11:00 anchor said, in his stentorian voice, "a man walking
his dog made a grisly discovery today in the small village
of Grosvenor, New Jersey. We'll go live now to the scene
of this heinous crime that has upset an entire town. B.J.?"

The news camera showed a reporter, B.J. Waters, standing in front of some bushes. It could have been anywhere,
but of course viewers knew where this particular clump of
bushes was, since the name of the town was flashed on the
screen.

"John," she said, as if this were a personal conversation
between herself and the news anchor, "I'm standing here
where only hours ago a resident along this quiet suburban
street found the body of an eighteen-year-old college freshman from upstate New York, who had only been attending
St. Michael's University here in Grosvenor for a short time.
Police aren't releasing his name, pending the notification
of his next of kin." She paused for a moment to look at
her notes.

"It appears from the preliminary reports that he was
stabbed in the chest. You can't see it in the studio, or at
home," she added, suddenly including the viewers in on the

story, "because it won't show on camera, but given the amount of blood on the ground where the body was found, he apparently bled to death."

A file film bearing the inscription *Earlier* along the top left-hand corner showed an ambulance and a body bag on a stretcher being put inside it. The tape played until the doors were shut and the ambulance drove away. All the while, a voice-over explained everything that was happening. The scene with the body bag was repeated twice, almost leading the audience to believe that there was more than one body, perhaps because there wasn't enough footage to fill the length of the narration.

Following that footage, various people were interviewed, all expressing shock, and the local police chief was seen and heard promising to wrap up the case quickly. Then the camera switched back to the live feed, with the appropriate designation for the viewers, and B.J.'s face was in the lights again, to further explain to the audience what they saw.

She interviewed a few passersby or, more accurately, people who had been lured out of their warm houses by the lights of the cameras and rescue vehicles. "Did you know the victim?" she asked each one.

"I've seen him walking along this street several times," one lady said. "I live in that house over there." She pointed, but the camera did not pan around to the house. "He was a nice boy. It's such a shame." The camera went in for a close up on her sad face, then switched back to the reporter.

"As you have just heard, police have no leads at this time, and it is a terrible shock to this small quiet town in suburban Essex County, which has seldom seen violence within its borders. We'll keep you updated if anything else breaks during this newscast." The serious, earnest look on her face was replaced by a big flashy smile. "Back to you, John."

The camera was back on the anchor's face. In his customary attempt to guide his viewers from one story to another, he went into his contrived segue. "Well, B.J.," he said, as if she were still listening, "it wasn't murder, but there was a big story today in another town in our viewing area . . ."

Nate turned off the TV. Fighting tears, Wally wrapped as much of her tiny frame as she could around her husband, considering how much taller he was, and tried to sleep, with little success.

Chapter Two

"A hundred twenty-five years," Captain Jaeger said between clenched teeth, when the two bleary-eyed young detectives arrived in his office the following morning. He motioned for them to take seats in the worn leather chairs in front of his desk and put down his copy of the file. "A hundred twenty-five years since this town was incorporated and I get to have the first murder. I can't believe this. The mayor is ready to kill me. They'll never get that blue ribbon now."

"Yes, sir," Elliot Levine said, who knew all about it, as did every person within earshot of His Honor. The town council had been applying for the award every year for the past four years, and the mayor had become more obnoxious with each lost bid. The entire squad room had been able to hear him yelling at the captain, as if the captain had stabbed the victim himself.

Jaeger sipped his coffee, visibly trying to calm himself. "We have to find out who did this."

Despite the tired face Elliot had seen in the mirror of the men's room while he tried to scrub the sleepiness off, he remained alert. Trying to conceal his excitement about possibly being allowed to continue working on the case, he glanced at his partner.

Dominique Scott nodded at Elliot before turning her gorgeous brown face back to their boss. Both had been up nearly all night gathering information on the murder. "We'll help the county find the killer," she said. "It's too bad we can't handle this on our own."

"You know we don't have the facilities or manpower, Scott," Jaeger said. "If you wanted to work on cases like that you should have taken a job with the county."

Dominique did not respond to his taunt, but clenched her long, slender fingers into balls. Elliot sent her a look of support, as much as he could manage, as exhausted as he was. It had been a long night.

As soon as the body was discovered and the murder reported to 911, the information was relayed state-wide on SPEN, the state police emergency network. But it was clear from the initial reports made by the first officer on the scene that they were probably too late. Whoever did it was most likely long gone. The body was getting cold, and so was the trail.

Elliot and Dominique had stayed with the forensics people and kept track of all the data collected. Captain Overbearing, as many of the officers called him, wanted to be told everything.

"I see that we don't have much to go on," Jaeger continued, after he read the list of items found at the scene. "It could have been worse, I suppose. It could have been a local resident. An out-of-towner isn't quite as bad."

The detectives did not say anything.

Jaeger looked at them. "We don't need this hanging over our heads. I only hope it was another outsider who did this."

Elliot marveled at his boss's lack of compassion. But he understood it. No one wanted to believe that anything like this could have happened in this town, but since it had, it would be better if it was done by and to outsiders. Besides, it was well known that Jaeger was eyeing the police director's job, and did not want an open case hanging over his head.

The only thing was, Elliot had never worked on a murder case before. Neither had his partner. Yet they were the ones the captain assigned to the case.

Jaeger handed them another folder. "I want you to read this file too. It just came up. You may have heard about it. Take a few minutes to get yourself up to speed. It may be something. Or it could just be another self-absorbed teenager who forgot to call her mother." He waited as they stood up to leave. "You could learn something from the murder investigation. Keep your hands in there and keep me posted."

They were nearly out the door when he added, "Report back to me in an hour. We'll go over everything." He stabbed his index finger in the air. "I don't want to be shut out on this."

"Can they do that, sir?" Elliot asked.

"If we let them. Or if we screw up. Don't screw up."

Wally deposited a bag of groceries on her back porch with a thud. After unlocking the back door, she picked up the bag and, carefully balancing another bundle in her left arm while not being able to see over the top of either bag, pushed her way into the kitchen. She had to force her black, tail-wagging, always-hungry, Labrador retriever out of the way, but spoke soothingly to him to make up for her rudeness.

"Just let me pass, Sammy, sweetie," she cooed. "I brought you some treats and I'll give them to you as soon as I unpack this bag."

After she hung her coat on its hook and straightened her sweater above her navy corduroy walking shorts, she got to work on putting everything away. The dog put his paws up on the counter and sniffed at the paper bags. Wally shooed him down as she pushed his enormous bag of dog food aside and placed the box of large-size dog biscuits into the spot on the shelf that they always occupied. Sammy lay down on the terra-cotta tile floor right in front of the oak cabinet, with his face between his paws and his eyebrows moving as he watched every move his mistress made.

As she struggled to get the new bag of flour onto its shelf, Wally wished for the seventh time that morning, and at least the six billionth time in her life, that she were taller. At only 4' 11", many things were out of her reach, like the shelf. It took a show of self-discipline for her to overcome her stubborn streak and pull the step stool out from under the kitchen sink.

Wally wasn't paying much attention to her groceries, because she was wondering about the horrible thing that had happened only a few blocks from her house. Everyone at the bank and the store had talked about it. Although much smaller occurrences could cause almost as much talk and even heated debate in the little town, this was really serious. She had never considered her town anything other than a safe haven, but now, with the murder of that poor college student, she was not so sure.

Two of the mothers dropping off their children at the nursery school where Wally taught had taken her aside to ask her how to handle the news of the murder and what to say to their kids. For the moment, Wally advised them not to bring it up, but if one of the children did, she advised the parent to be honest, reassuring and calm. The conversation had redirected her attention back into the world of crayons, apple juice, sticky fingers, and bathroom humor. Fifteen sweet, adorable, innocent children kept her busy and smiling, just as they and their predecessors had for over thirteen years.

The moment school was over, however, Wally went back to thinking about the murder.

When she went to put the milk into the refrigerator, she noticed that there was a box of cereal on the shelf. For a person who paid attention to every detail, it was almost unbelievable. She realized just how out of it she had been at breakfast. Her lack of sleep was showing and she was glad that no one was home to see her mistake. That included Nate.

He had advised her not to think about the murder and told her that whatever she wanted to do to help, she should forget. Wally knew that he wasn't being selfish—his charitable nature would never allow that—but he felt that there was nothing she could do to fix the problem. Yet she couldn't get it out of her mind.

As soon as she was done with the groceries, she gave Sammy a dog biscuit and checked the answering machine on the wall next to where she had hung her jacket. In all likelihood there would be no messages. Nate was in his office just up the driveway at this time of day and would have answered the house line if it had rung. The red light stared back at her unblinkingly, just as she expected.

It was not quite 1:00, and she had managed to do all of the errands in less than the hour it had been since the children in school went home. She still had time to check the mail. Since it was a Thursday, the local newspaper with its week-old news, gossip and propaganda would have arrived.

Wally snatched it up and looked for the pictures of her nursery students walking to the library. It was on the first page, and showed the children holding loops of a rope as they crossed the street. The photographer had carefully written down all the children's names when he snapped the photo, but as Wally read the caption she was disappointed.

According to the newspaper, the picture was of a day care center's autumn walk in the park. "How typical," Wally said to no one, since no one was home. She wondered if she should call the newspaper and have them print a correction, but knew it might take weeks, if it ever happened, and would just be an annoying loose end she was waiting to tie up.

But as she turned to go back to the kitchen, something caught her eye. She wasn't alone in the house. Nate lay sprawled on the plush, white carpet of the living room, with his face up, his arms folded across his chest, and his eyes closed.

Chapter Three

"**Y**ou look like something that washed up on the beach," Wally said with a giggle, as she looked through the rest of the mail. Nate actually looked more like the sky at the beach. He wore a light blue v-neck sweater that brought out the blue side of his blue-green eyes and a pair of faded but neat looking jeans. Even the button-down shirt under his sweater was a pale blue and white stripe. To Wally he looked wonderful, especially with his hair so nicely turning more silvery each year, but his expression said otherwise. She went over to stand above him. "Does your back still hurt?"

"Hm," Nate mumbled.

"I told you not to plant those shrubs," she said, while sifting through the letters and advertisements. She tossed anything bearing her legal name, Voltairine, into the trash unopened, after only the briefest glance. The only reason she even looked at letters like that was to avoid a repetition of the time she threw away her new driver's license because it had her real name on it. The DMV had taken six weeks to send her another one, giving her more grief than it was worth. "The planting could have waited until the weekend, when Mark comes home," she told her husband.

Nate rolled over and got into a sitting position, using the bench from the family-photo-laden baby grand piano to assist him. "Then why did you buy them last week?"

Wally stared at her husband, thinking that he should know perfectly well why she bought them when she did, but not saying it. Kicking off her bright red loafers so that she could walk on the carpet had left her standing in her navy tights, even tinier next to her tall husband. Although she was small, she was strong, and she helped him stand up, taking care to be gentle.

Nate waited expectantly for an answer, so she tried to explain it again. "Because they were on sale and I didn't want to risk having them be sold out."

Regardless of the fact that it was his own fault, Wally felt sorry that her husband was so achy. Reaching around behind him, she rubbed his back and shoulders. Nate's lean, strong body felt good, even under his sweater. "You're sure it was the planting that did this?"

"Of course. Why do you ask?"

Wally looked at his face, suntanned even this late in the season. "You don't think it may have had something to do with your playing golf right afterward, and tennis the next morning, and wasn't that you I saw getting up at six this morning to go play racquetball?"

"Um," Nate said, smiling sheepishly. "Exercise is good for my back. Planting isn't."

"Too old, huh?" Wally teased. She knew he would never admit to that, irrespective of the fact that he had just celebrated his fiftieth birthday, and she was right.

Nate shook his head. "Anyone at any age could get a backache, you know."

Wally shrugged and led the way to the kitchen. "Would you like some soup?"

"Sure." Nate gingerly sat his tall frame down in one of

the ladder-back kitchen chairs and rested against it, gazing out through the large windows of the attached garden room. The yard was covered with multi-colored leaves from the large trees that lined the driveway.

Wally defrosted a container of soup from her freezer and put it into a pot to finish heating. Putting aside her musings, she set the pot on a burner, adjusted the heat, and made tuna sandwiches.

She set lunch on the table, then picked up the remote control and aimed it at the television in the adjoining room.

"What are you doing?"

"I taped the noon news."

She disregarded her husband's puzzlement, pressed rewind, then hit play.

It seemed that nothing much else was happening in the whole tri-state area, because the murder of the St. Michael's University student topped the news. Wally watched in awe as her town, her neighborhood, appeared on the screen.

"Coming up, murder in suburban New Jersey," the voice-over said, with the noon news music playing its frenetic tune in the background. Pictures of people walking on the sidewalk near a car accident filled the screen, with the explanation that yet another New York City cab had jumped the curb. "But first we'll see what people on the street have to say about this constant menace," said the voice. "Weather and sports, all on Eyewitness News at Noon."

After the commercials, two lovely faces appeared on the screen. They were the noon news anchors. The blond blue-eyed one on the left introduced herself and welcomed the other, a brown-eyed brunet.

She began to speak. "Police this noon still have no leads on the brutal slaying of a young college student from upstate New York, whose body was found in Grosvenor, New Jersey, last night. It was the first murder in the history of the town."

File film flashed across the screen and the previous evening's tapes were run. A reporter, the same as the night before, had been sent out to cover the story in daylight. "B.J. Waters joins us now at the site of this grisly discovery."

Little could be seen on the screen of the actual crime scene. Yellow police tape seemed to have been strung all around the bushes. Many people stood nearby, some of whom Wally recognized. It made her shiver. She had specifically avoided the area on her errands, but here it was, right in her home, on the news.

B.J. Waters did not have much to say regarding the crime, although she did have the name of the victim. "Young Brian Lambert, the only child of a widow from upstate New York, could not have been in town for more than two and a half months," she read from her notes. "Yet he met with a horrible fate last evening on this quiet stretch of road in this small town. Police aren't saying if they have any leads in the case but teachers and friends at St. Michael's University are being questioned. Mr. Lambert's landlady, who rented him a room in her house, has declined comment." She paused while a picture of a police captain was shown, obviously refusing to speak to the reporters who all pushed microphones into his face.

"We'll be following this story all day if necessary," B.J. Waters said, when the short tape had finished, "and will update you as soon as we hear anything. We expect a press conference around three o'clock, which we will bring to you live." She paused, closing her notebook, and smiled. "Back to you in the newsroom."

Wally turned off the VCR and television. Both she and her husband were quiet as they ate.

"I heard from Renee Nichols again today," Nate said after a while, wiping his mouth with a napkin.

"How soon can she get her check?"

"I'm about to file the paperwork. The car has been missing without a trace for almost the full sixty days. I think even the carrier can pretty well assume that the car isn't coming back. That's when I'll forward the claim. She should get paid quickly."

Wally hoped that was true. Nate had told her what a big expense it was for his clients. Since Renee had to drive so many car-pools, she'd had to rent a mini-van to replace the Volvo wagon. The rental was very high, and the policy coverage didn't fully pay for the fees.

Nate had done the best he could, Wally knew, given the limitations on the policy. She was proud of how committed her husband was to the side business he'd inherited from his father when his parents moved to Florida. Even though he was more interested in his own investment business, he'd moved the insurance agency into the barn behind the house, the only one still standing for miles around, along with a yearly intern to spare him from the humdrum boring stuff that would drive him up the walls. While he didn't actively seek out new customers, he treated those that he had well.

Nate finished his coffee, kissed Wally, and reached for his jacket. With a wave, he and Sammy, who had a play corner in the office, headed for the barn. He was about halfway up the driveway when the office phone rang. Rather than let the machine in the barn pick up, since she did not think that Nate would catch it in time, Wally decided to answer the house extension.

She picked it up and said, "Morris and Company."

"Is that you, Wally?" an agitated voice asked. "I thought I dialed the house."

"It's okay, Louise," Wally said. "It's just one number different. How are you?"

Louise Fisch, Wally's best friend, was often excitable, and Wally assumed that her tone of voice was due to the mistake with the phone number, or maybe the news of the murder. But what Louise said chilled Wally. "Terrible. Lori Kaufman is missing!"

Chapter Four

The image of the little four-year-old girl Lori had been when Wally taught her first nursery school class popped into her mind. Lori was older now, of course, but the thought of her being missing scared Wally. "What do you mean, missing?"

"Lori didn't come home from practice last night," Louise explained, her usually jovial voice shrill. "She was with all the other girls when they left at six o'clock. Her mother thought she was going to a friend's house to do her home-work, but her friend called at about seven, saying that she'd gotten finished with the dentist early, and asking if she could come over." Louise stopped to take a breath, but immediately continued. "Her mother had thought the girls were together, and she became frantic and called me and everyone else she knew. But no one had seen her. So then they called the police, who, if you'll remember, were kind of busy last night. When she didn't get home by morning the police finally said they'd do something about it."

Wally followed Louise's story in shock. She had not seen the Kaufman girl very much since nursery school, although she had seen her at football games when Mark marched in the band. Lori was a year behind Mark in school, and was a cheerleader. And she knew Lori's parents, because both Lori and her younger sister, Felice, had been students in Wally's class several years apart. Sandy Kaufman was a very nice woman, and it tore at Wally's heart that her daughter was missing.

"Did the police find anything?" Wally asked. "I haven't read anything about it in the newspapers."

"No!" Louise said. "They haven't found a thing. There could be a kidnapper loose."

A shiver passed down Wally's spine. "Why do you say that?"

"You know Lori. Maybe not as well as I do." Louise's tone narrowly missed sounding like she was a know-it-all, but Wally knew her best friend better and chalked it up to distress. "We've stayed friendly with her and her mother since the day Lori and my daughter started school together. She'd never run away."

Wally had not even suggested that, and thought it unlikely, based on what she knew of Lori's mother, but she knew it was a possibility that had to be considered. "Had she been having any trouble lately? Like at school, or home, or maybe with a boy?"

"Of course not. Sandy would have told me. Everything was perfect. She was getting applications ready for college."

"So what are they doing about it?" Wally asked. The local police force had no experience dealing with anything like this, just as it had no experience dealing with the murder. They would be overwhelmed in no time. In the calm town of Grosvenor, not much ever happened. It had its share of the usual car thefts, and an occasional tragic accident, but never any major crime before yesterday. Now there seemed to be two.

"I don't really know," Louise said. "There was no ransom note or anything with instructions about not involving the police, and the whole thing could be public, but it won't be, because they are trying to keep it out of the papers and off the television. There is enough about the town in the papers today anyway, none of it good."

Wally agreed, although she realized that some people in Louise's position would be worrying about the lingering impact that these crimes, even after they were solved, would have on the real estate market in the town. Louise was the top real estate agent in her office. But Wally knew her friend better than that. She had a huge heart and it sounded like it was breaking.

"There are counselors working at the high school," Louise said, sniffling, "to help the kids with their emotions, and parents have been advised to be very careful. The school started the phone chain, and that's when I realized that Lori still hadn't turned up. I just don't know what to do."

"Stay by the phone and let me know if you hear anything," Wally said, as she loaded the last of the lunch dishes into the dishwasher.

Once she finished talking to Louise it was time for action. Wally could not get her thoughts off the two incidents. What bothered her most was that the murder and Lori's disappearance kept merging together in her mind. She had formed a plan and was ready to go.

Wally darted into the nearby bathroom and brushed her hair, attempting as usual to get the left side to bend under at her chin the way the right side did. Opening her big freezer, she pulled out a vegetarian lasagna she had planned to serve over the weekend. It would be more useful today, she decided, as she threw on her coat. Lori's family might need it.

There was usually extra food in the Morris freezer because whenever she cooked she also prepared for unknown contingencies. As a result, Wally had quite a reputation for always being able to throw together a full meal, even on short notice.

Besides the lasagna, she took out a marble loaf cake she had recently bought at the bake sale on election day, thinking that maybe the Kaufmans would like that too.

Quickly, before going out to her car, she called Nate at the office and told him what was happening. "Be careful," he warned. "Let me know if I can help."

Wally blew a kiss into the phone, and left the house, forgetting to look up the address. Luckily, she kept an old copy of the town phone book in her new white Lexus. It turned out that they did not live far away. Wally probably could have walked, since she walked further than that just for exercise, especially since it was on one of the few level roads in the town. But she had things to carry, so she started the engine, backed down the driveway away from the old barn where Nate had his office, and pulled into the street.

The Kaufmans' house was five blocks down on the main road, with no parking allowed out front, so Wally had to pull her car around the corner to park. She picked up her packages and walked up to their door.

It seemed so strange that this attractive gray house with the black shutters that she had passed so many times before should have such trouble. It looked the same as it always did when she went by, but the red front door, usually closed this time of day, was open, with only the storm door shut.

Wally rang the bell, and waited. She heard shuffling and then running; it was the sound of a frenzied mother running to see if her missing child had returned.

The sun was behind Wally, and Sandy blinked several times, as if she was having trouble recognizing her visitor. Then she opened the storm door, pushing it outward.

Wally stepped back to get out of the way. "I'm so sorry," she said. "I brought you some food. I thought it might be useful."

Although she appeared distracted, Sandy motioned for Wally to come in.

"Thank you," Sandy said, as she put the frozen containers on the counter in the kitchen.

"You're welcome. I didn't want to bother you, but if I can help . . ." There was no way to finish that sentence. Both women were too close to tears.

Lori's mother seemed determined to fight them off. As she put the lasagna into her refrigerator she indicated that Wally should sit at the kitchen table. Sandy went about the business of making coffee and taking down mugs from the shelf near the coffee maker. But when she turned back toward her guest, Wally could see that her face was red and her eyes were puffy. Her shoulder-length brown hair was usually one of her better features. Wally noted that today it was loosely tied back with a plain rubber band, and she wore jeans and a sweatshirt that had a stain on the front. Although it made Wally feel a little embarrassed for not having called before coming over, in the circumstances she did not think that would have changed much. It was unlikely that Sandy would have gone to the trouble to fix herself up.

"How's Mark doing?" Sandy asked, her voice tight. "He's in his first year at Princeton, right?"

"Yes. He's fine. He'll be home this weekend." Wally shivered, thinking about another college freshman, now dead.

"That's nice." Sandy took a deep breath. "And I heard that Debbie started law school."

Wally nodded. Her middle child had made her and Nate proud when she announced that she would not only go to law school, but pay for it herself.

The conversation rattled Wally. Although she felt that they should be discussing Lori, there didn't seem to be any way to bring it up. There was an uncomfortable silence.

"I heard you became a grandmother," Sandy said. "You seem too young."

Wally laughed. She brushed her hand self-consciously through her chin length hair, and gave a tug to the uncooperative left side. What Sandy had said was true; although she was almost within shouting distance of fifty, Wally sometimes still got mistaken for a child. But it was also true that her eldest, Rachel, had a baby girl. She was a pink and white, blue-eyed, strawberry-blond cutie-pie named Jody.

Wally wanted to steer the conversation back to Lori, but it was so difficult. "Felice . . . ?"

Sandy sat down opposite Wally. "She'd love to see you, but she's . . ." She looked up at the ceiling, then back to Wally. "She won't talk to anyone. Lori is her whole world. Felice looks up to her big sister. Maybe I should . . ."

Wally put her hand on Sandy's shoulder. "Don't bother her. I'm sure it will be okay," she said. "They'll find Lori, and everything will be fine." *If only that's true*, Wally thought, as she explained how to heat the lasagna. "Don't worry about the pan," she said. "It's disposable."

"I wish we heard something," said Sandy. "If we knew that someone had her, that she was safe. But we don't know anything."

"Tell me what happened," Wally said.

"I've told the police this about ten times. Lori came home after school, like she always does, and started her homework. But she had to go back for cheerleading practice. That's the last I saw of her." She began to cry. "We know she got to practice all right, but she never came home again." Sandy paused, trying to prevent her voice from cracking, but she was unsuccessful. "I didn't even realize she was missing until Jackie called to ask if she could come over, and I'd thought she had been with Jackie the whole time."

"Jackie?" Wally asked. "Jackie Gibson?"

"Yes."

Wally knew that Lori Kaufman and Jackie Gibson were almost always together, even though Jackie was from the other side of the town. It was not a very big town, and everyone went to the same high school.

"Jackie hadn't seen her for at least an hour when I found out," Sandy said. "Lori was missing for a long time, and here I sat, merrily reading a magazine while dinner cooked, and she was out there with who knows what."

"You mustn't blame yourself," Wally said.

They were interrupted by the doorbell. Sandy pushed back her chair and ran to the front door. Wally followed, and what she saw scared her nearly to death. There was a police car parked where no other car could legally park, right in front of the house. There were also two police officers on the front stoop, detectives showing their badges and giving their names, which immediately went out of Wally's head as she waited to hear what they had to say.

Chapter Five

"**H**ave you found her?" asked Sandy, straining to look beyond the officers into their car.

"May we come in?" the female officer asked. She rested her hand tentatively on the storm door's knob.

"Oh, God!" Sandy cried, sinking onto the sofa.

The young woman held up her other hand. "No, we haven't found anything. It isn't that. Please," she said loudly through the glass, "let us come in and explain."

Wally opened the door for them and turned to Sandy. "Should I leave you alone to talk?"

Sandy shook her head, as she watched the police officers walk past them into the living room. "Please don't go. It's good to have you here with me. Jeff has been walking the streets since last night."

The second detective stood in front of the large picture window. Because of the glare of the sun behind him, Wally could not see his face. He cleared his throat. "It's okay with us if you stay, Mrs. Morris."

Wally was startled that the detective knew her name. She moved around the room over to the side of the couch, to look at him more closely without the sun behind him. Looking way up into his face, since he was quite tall and she was so short, she saw familiar intense blue eyes in a boyishly handsome face. His curly light brown hair was trimmed much shorter than the last time she saw him but she had no trouble recognizing him. "Elliot?"

"Yes, ma'am?"

The urge to run over and hug this boy who had been a classmate and good friend of Rachel's in high school almost overwhelmed Wally. But she resisted. It was hardly the time for a reunion. She vaguely remembered reading that some officers had been hired to fill detective positions that had opened up on the force. Although she had not bothered reading their names, she was certain that was how Elliot had come to be standing in Sandy's living room. It was wonderful that he was working on the case, she thought. He was a very bright boy.

"Did anyone see Lori last night?"

"No one has come forward," the female officer, Dominique Scott, said. To Wally she looked like a model, even though she was only about five-five, not what Wally would have expected for a female police officer. Her beautiful dark face and eyes were framed by neatly combed black hair pulled back into a professional-looking French braid. "And we have to be very careful about publicly asking for assistance because we are keeping a news blackout on Lori's disappearance, as you requested," she added

Wally felt the young detective was right about the news, and it was a relief to hear about the blackout since the recent efforts of several people to swamp the airwaves and newspapers in search of their missing children had not proven successful. The image of Lori's face being plastered on television was frightening and the thought of her story being mentioned over and over every few minutes on the all-news radio stations made Wally's skin prickle.

The front door opened, letting in a rush of chilly air. Jeff

Kaufman came in, looking cold, tired, and stiff. He also looked terrified, Wally guessed, because of the police car out front.

"What's going on?" he asked, seeing his living room filled with people. In a shaky voice, he added, "Did you find her?"

"No, sir," Elliot said. Wally left him to explain, and went with Sandy into the kitchen to get some tea and food for Jeff.

"I don't know how we are going to handle it if anything happens to Lori," Sandy said.

Wally felt waves of compassion wash over her, and she was relieved that even though she wasn't close friends with the Kaufman family, she was available for them to lean on. "I'm certain she'll be fine," Wally said. Yet she could not help feeling that every passing minute was a sign of disaster.

She drove home in a daze, unable to get the picture of Sandy and Jeff sitting miserably at their kitchen table out of her mind. That such a horrible thing could happen in the town was unbelievable. She passed the same parks as always, all bathed in bright sunshine, but they seemed to have a hard, unfriendly edge to them.

Something bothered her about the conversation with the police. The possibility was strong that the death of the young man might be connected to Lori's disappearance. She wondered if their search of the murder scene would yield any clues about Lori.

She turned her car right on the next corner and went around the block. After winding her way down to the bottom of the street, she turned left and went back toward the little brook that ran along the road in the middle of an old residential area. Most of the houses in this area were big, and were primarily Federal and Dutch Colonial in design. At this time of year they looked somewhat golden-brown as the last of the leaves carpeted their lawns, and the withering remains of Halloween pumpkins smiled crookedly from the front stoops.

Many houses lined the street, all seeming to slope into the hill, with one side being higher than the other in order for the insides of the houses to be level. Each of the ones on the west side of the road had a small bridge over the driveway to let the water of the brook pass underneath.

The houses were spaced evenly, some visible to each other, but there was one short stretch where the road curved sharply and headed upward. The bushes and trees on the north side almost obscured the view of the south side of the road. Every few years someone mounted a protest because it was a driving hazard when the bushes were too high. A small army from the parks department would come and trim them close to the ground. Wally guessed that the following summer would be about the time to cut them back again.

She pulled over and parked her car, being careful to set her hand brake and make sure she was not on a pile of leaves. Nate had warned her about that many times. He had processed several claims over the years for cars that had caught fire from leaves underneath. She would never live it down if her car self-immolated and became one of his statistics.

When she got out, she looked around the bushes, hoping to find something that might lead to a link between Lori and Brian. But aside from a flattened area surrounded by police tape, she did not see much. There were many footprints and it was clear that the police and several onlookers had examined the street.

The light was beginning to fade. It had also turned colder. Nate would be waiting. Wally got back in her car and headed home. But Lori's disappearance and that poor boy's death nagged at her. She hated loose ends and these were loose ends of the worst kind. And terrifying.

* * *

The evening news was bleak. All the networks carried pictures of poor Brian Lambert's mother and a woman identified as his aunt Celia being led out of the police station. Reporters were seen attempting to talk to her, to intrude on her grief, a grief Wally could feel right through the television. She hated that kind of thing. It was so maudlin.

In contrast to the latest trend in interviews of a victim's family, Brian's mother and aunt remained silent. There was not even a family spokesperson to explain Mrs. Lambert's feelings. Personally, Wally thought Mrs. Lambert's feelings were obvious. And very sad.

Chapter Six

On Friday, Timmy Parsons's mother was late picking him up. As so often happened, she called the school at 11:55 and told them she was on her way. That meant that she would be there no sooner than 12:30.

Wally held Timmy's hand as the other children were picked up. He squeezed hers tightly, and sniffled.

"Your mom will be here soon," Wally said. The little boy nodded, but he didn't seem convinced.

The last child was picked up, and her mother lowered the passenger side window and waved at Wally. "Do you want me to take him? They live nearby. I told his mother I could always bring him home."

Knowing that Timmy's mother was on the way, and also that his information card specifically prohibited anyone from taking Timmy from the school, Wally shook her head. "His mom will be here soon. But thanks."

Timmy watched the car drive off. "Do you want to go inside?" Wally asked. "It's a little cold out here."

He nodded. They went back to the classroom. Wally read to the little boy until his mother came, frantic as usual.

"I tried to get away," she explained, re-zipping Timmy's jacket. "It's just so hard."

"Cara's mother offered to take him home. She could drop him off with the baby sitter. Then you wouldn't have to leave work."

"I can't do that. No one else can drive him. I have to be sure."

Wally decided that there was no point in arguing, particularly in front of Timmy. The woman had her reasons. It was really a pity.

When Wally got home, she called the police station and asked to speak to Elliot Levine. She wanted to see if there was any news.

They talked for a while, catching up on Elliot's life since high school, and Rachel's, since they had been friendly back then.

Finally the conversation turned to Lori's disappearance. "I wondered if there was any connection to that poor college student," Wally said.

"Most likely none," Elliot told her. "Why would you think so?"

"He was found along Brookside Lane, and Sandy said that was the route that Lori would take to go home from the high school."

Elliot sighed. "We aren't even sure how long he was there, or what time he was stabbed."

"Did anyone report him missing before he was found?"

"Not according to our records," Elliot said. "His landlady said she never keeps close tabs on her tenants. They are adults, in her eyes."

Wally bristled at the woman's lack of interest. "Did you find anything on Lori?"

Elliot explained that they had not found any leads on the teenager yet, and, though the county and state had promised to help where they could on the disappearance, they were still searching alone. They had briefly questioned all of Lori's friends, but no one knew anything.

Before Wally could ask another question, Elliot said, "I really shouldn't be talking about the investigation."

"It's only to me. I won't tell anyone. I was just trying to help."

"This is a job for the police."

"Can't you tell me anything?"

"You aren't going to let me get off the phone until I tell you about it, are you?"

"Probably not, if I can help it."

After a short pause, Elliot admitted that there were some things he could tell her without compromising the investigation. "Her friend Jackie was really upset. Much more so than the other girls."

"They are best friends," Wally said, by way of explanation.

"I know they're very close, but I couldn't help getting the feeling that she felt helpless in some way."

"We all are, I guess. I feel somewhat helpless myself, and I know that Lori's parents do too."

Elliot was quiet for a minute. "I can't explain it, but there seemed to be something else. She doesn't know anything, she says, but her face was . . . I don't know how to define it. Yet we've verified that she was at the dentist when Lori disappeared, so I guess it's just my imagination."

"I didn't want to ask Sandy this," Wally said. "But is there a boyfriend who might be involved?"

"We are looking into that too. Mrs. Kaufman told us that Lori was very popular, but happens to be between boyfriends right now."

"So did you question the one she most recently broke up with?"

"We are tracking him down."

Wally decided to try a different tack, and get closer to

what she most wondered about. "Did you find anything on Brookside Lane or Porridge Lane?"

"No," Elliot said. "I don't know why you think the murder is related to Lori."

"Think about it. Two terrible things happen in a place that never has these things happen. Do you honestly think there is no connection?"

There was a silence on the other end of the line. Elliot broke it with a mumbled response.

"What did you find?" Wally asked, pressing now.

"Just smashed bushes, and some of Brian Lambert's belongings. There was a backpack, a few pens, and a calculator, which may have fallen out of his pockets."

"Did you search the whole street?"

"What do you mean?" Elliot's voice sounded annoyed that Wally would question his professionalism.

"I just meant that maybe there might have been something further down the road."

"Why do you think that?" Elliot asked. "There were no drag marks or anything to indicate he'd been moved. He died where he was stabbed, according to the evidence."

"I was going over it in my mind. If Lori was involved and was taken by someone, she'd try to get away. Maybe she ran onto the lawn of someone's house, trying to get help."

"We questioned all the neighbors. No one heard or saw anything. And believe me, as hard as it was, we searched the whole town for her body, just in case." Elliot's voice held more than a trace of impatience. "I have to go, Mrs. Morris."

"One more question, Elliot. I promise," she said. "Did you go far up or down the road, in both directions, to see if maybe, if Lori was pulled into a car or something, she tried to get out? Maybe there might be some clues further away from that clump of bushes, like, well, like I don't know, but maybe."

This time Elliot was quiet for a long time. Wally was getting ready to stress what she saw as an obvious connection and explain what she meant, when he said, "Maybe we should go look."

"Can I come along?" Wally asked. "I can help."

"Uh, no, that wouldn't be right," Elliot said.

"Will you tell me if you find anything?"

"If I can," Elliot said. "I can't promise."

After Wally hung up, she got lunch ready for herself and Nate. When she was done, she looked up and saw her husband walking down the driveway from the barn. Sammy followed behind him, darting off every few feet to explore the surroundings. Poor dog. There was so much to sniff out there, and so little time.

"I tried to call," Nate said. The dog pushed past him as he came inside, and gave Wally a big greeting, wagging his long stiff tail wildly. "Who were you talking to?"

Wally reached her face up to Nate's for a kiss. "Elliot. Did you want something special?"

"Oh." He seemed to be trying to gauge her mood. Finally he asked, "Did they find Lori?"

"No. Not yet," she added, in a effort to sound positive.

"That's a shame," Nate said, lightening his tone, although Wally could tell that he was really worried. None of his familiar laugh lines showed, and his brow was deeply furrowed. She wished she could see him smile, just for reassurance.

"I wondered when lunch was," he said, "that's all. I knew you were busy today."

She didn't believe it for a minute, but she played along. "Lunch is all ready."

The phone rang just as they finished eating. Elliot's voice sounded almost apologetic. "Mrs. Morris? We found something."

Wally froze. "What?"

"As you suggested, we searched all the way up Porridge

Lane and then back down the other way. We found a set of keys and I'm going over to the Kaufmans to see if they recognize them. I was wondering if you'd go with us, to help out."

"Sure," Wally said. "I can be there in fifteen minutes."

"Thanks. We'll meet you outside." Elliot hung up.

She drove the few short blocks to Sandy's, not even feeling guilty about not walking. The weather, a chilling drizzle, was too nasty anyway. She arrived just as Elliot and his partner drove up.

Sandy's face was devoid of color when she opened the door, and as they went inside, she hung heavily on Wally's arm. "Jeff isn't home," she explained. "He's out looking for her again. I don't even know where he's going. She can't be anywhere in town." She sat down on one flowered sofa, and told Elliot and his partner to sit on the love seat opposite her. All the while she chattered, obviously trying to avoid seeing what Elliot had called to say he wanted to show her. "They had to ask him to leave the mall last night. He checked all the stores, showing her picture all around, but no one had seen her and he was scaring customers."

Wally privately doubted that any storekeeper would be likely to remember a particular teenager. But she didn't say anything.

Elliot pulled a plastic bag out of his pocket and placed it on the coffee table between them. Inside was a set of keys. He held them up, still inside the bag, for Sandy to see.

"Oh!" she cried. "Those are Lori's!"

"Are you sure?" Detective Scott asked.

"Yes, of course," Sandy said. "That's the key to the top lock, and this other one is to the bottom." She showed them which was which, by turning the bag. "This one is for my car, and this one is for Jeff's. And this," she said, sniffling, "is her diary key. Where did you get these?"

"We found them near the corner of Porridge and Birchwood. They were on someone's lawn, in a pile of leaves, as if they were dropped there."

"Lori always keeps her keys in her hand when she is coming home," Sandy said. "Even if I'm with her, with my own keys."

"We think that maybe she dropped them there," Elliot explained, as if it were his idea to look. Wally did not say a word.

"Why would she do that?" Sandy asked.

"Maybe she was forced into a car and was trying to get out. She could have dropped or even thrown them," the female officer said. "We don't know. It may tell us which direction they were headed, assuming she was on the passenger side of the car, but which way they turned onto Porridge is still a question, as well as where they went from there."

"But," Elliot said, "it makes us reasonably sure that she didn't go of her own free will, that she didn't just run away."

"I knew she didn't run away," Sandy said. She began to cry again.

"Maybe there is something in her diary that would explain her disappearance," Wally suggested.

Elliot looked surprised but seemed to like the idea. "That's possible. Especially if someone was bothering her or making threats."

"She never mentioned it," Sandy said. "And she always told me everything."

Wally was skeptical about that, but said, "Maybe she thought it wasn't important."

"May we see that diary?" Officer Scott asked.

"I guess so." Sandy went upstairs and returned carrying a small red book with a strap and lock. She seemed reluctant to hand the diary over. "Will I get this back?"

Elliot assured her that they would return it. He and his partner left soon after, promising to stay in touch. Wally walked them to the door and watched through the window while they drove away, trying to gather strength to help her friend.

Sandy sat on the couch, hugging a framed black and white picture that she picked up off the baby grand piano. It was of Lori and another girl. Wally asked if she could see it.

"It's a good shot of both of them," Sandy said, handing it over. "It's Lori and Jackie, on the day they were named head cheerleaders. It's going to be in the yearbook. Originally it was published in the Weekly Record."

"It's lovely," Wally said.

"Lori wanted to be a cheerleader ever since she was a little girl," her mother said. "She took cheerleading classes at the Y when she was very small, and went to a mini-camp for cheerleading. For three straight Halloweens she dressed up as a cheerleader, first as one from my college, then Jeff's, and then the one here in town."

Wally remembered Lori wearing one of the outfits to nursery school every day for five weeks. She looked at the picture of the two girls again.

"You know, Jackie has been really upset by all of this," Sandy said. "Her mother said she couldn't go to school today. She calls every hour or so."

They were still talking when Jeff came back, sodden and half frozen. His blond-turning-to-gray hair was damp and he looked exhausted. Wally promised to be available whenever they needed her and put her coat on to leave. She felt that the Kaufmans should have some time to be alone.

Chapter Seven

Louise Fisch looked surprised to see Wally on the door-step of her Tudor house. "What are you doing here at this hour?" she asked. "Shouldn't you be home baking or something?"

"I just came back from Sandy's," Wally said. She looked at her good friend, and smiled, as usual.

Louise always made her smile, with her thousands of freckles and long, bright-red hair, which was now pulled back in a ponytail. Usually funny and sweet, today she seemed very upset. "I thought she wouldn't want a million people trooping through her house, so I stayed away." She sounded hurt.

"No," Wally reassured her. "It isn't anything like that. I've been trying to help. I brought her some food yesterday. I didn't think she'd want to cook."

"Oh, you and your overstocked freezer. Always trying to take care of the whole world. I keep telling you that you can't do it all, but then you just go ahead and sign yourself up to do something else." She tugged on Wally's arm, pulling her into the house. "Well, come in and tell me all about

38

Sandy and why you were there today. Decaf okay?" She led the way into her lemon yellow kitchen, which nearly matched the turtleneck sweater she was wearing, where she poured out coffee for both of them.

"I didn't want to bother her," Louise explained. "That's why I didn't go over there."

"The rabbi said that in times of trouble we should get involved, not stay away."

"I must have missed that sermon," Louise said. "You were right to bring her food. It was a good idea. I'll do it for tonight's dinner after Michelle gets home, maybe a cooked chicken and whatever." That last part was said more to herself than to Wally, as if she was making a mental note.

"I'm sure she'll appreciate that," Wally said. "You've known her for a long time."

"Yes. Michelle and Lori were best friends since nursery school, as you might remember. That is, until Lori met Jackie."

The mention of Jackie's name piqued Wally's interest. "When was that, exactly?"

Louise had the look of a mother who has spent countless hours comforting a teary teenager. "The day they started high school. Jackie and Lori had gone to different middle schools but ended up in the same homeroom, and they had the same first period class. They got lost on the way, according to Michelle, and became friends while they were trying to find out where they were." She sighed. "Sometimes that happens, but Michelle was hurt because she felt pushed out. She couldn't compete with the two of them, especially since she's like this, and they . . ." With a gesture of her hands, she indicated that Michelle was much taller than the two petite cheerleaders. "They were so much alike." Instantly she put her hand to her mouth. "I didn't mean 'were!' "

"I know what you mean," Wally said. "Don't worry

about it. But it's odd that they never met before high school."

"Well," Louise explained, "Jackie's mother has always worked, so Jackie didn't take any after-school programs. Besides, they didn't always live in town. I think Michelle said that they moved in when Jackie was ten."

"I hadn't realized that Michelle knew Jackie that well."

"Oh, yes. Lori tried hard to keep the three of them together as friends. Michelle has been to Jackie's house many times, although not recently."

"Does she know where Jackie moved from?" Wally asked.

A door slammed, causing Louise to wince. "I think you can ask her yourself." Michelle walked into the kitchen, shedding her jacket and book bag onto the floor. Louise looked disgusted, but didn't ask her to pick it up. Wally knew the feeling.

"Hi. Ask me what?" the girl said. The plaid flannel shirt she wore over a t-shirt and jeans was unbuttoned and her long, thick, almost-orange hair hung loose. She pushed it back off her face and over her shoulder as she peered into the refrigerator.

"You can say hello to our guest," Louise said.

"Hi," Michelle said, turning her warm brown eyes toward Wally. Her fair-complexioned face, so like her mother's, was polite, but not in the least interested. Still, she had the manners to add, "How are you?"

"Very well, thank you," Wally said. "I was asking your mother about Jackie. She must be so upset."

"I guess so," Michelle said. "I haven't talked to her."

"Wally was wondering where Jackie moved from, before she came to live in town," said Louise.

"Oh, somewhere in the Midwest. She used to live on a farm, I think."

"Why do you say that?" her mother asked. "Not everyone in the Midwest lives on a farm, you know."

"I saw all the pictures of Jackie on a shelf in her living room. In two of them she was in front of a barn," Michelle said, with a smug, "so-there" smile on her face.

"I have a barn," Wally said, bending the left side of her hair under, with little success. The tension between Louise and her daughter was embarrassing, although all mothers of teenagers were familiar with it.

"Oh, I know that you have one," Michelle said, changing her tone to a more respectful one. Children generally did not use nasty tones on other people's parents, as Wally well knew.

"But there were horses and cows along the side of the barn," Michelle added. "And in one there was little Jackie with long pigtails sitting on an ugly little pony."

Wally nodded at Michelle. "I guess it was a farm."

"She lived in, uh, Nebraska, that's it. That was before her mother remarried and moved here." Michelle seemed disgusted by the topic. "Is it okay if I go now? I have a lot of homework and I want to go out tonight." She took a look at her mother's worried face and added, "Just to Julie's house."

"Sure, honey," Louise said.

Wally wanted to ask another question, and although she hated to overrule a parent, felt it was important. "Michelle, does Lori have a boyfriend who could be involved?"

The girl turned to her in surprise. "No. No one in school would do that."

"What about out of school, at St. Michael's for instance?"

"How did you know?"

Louise sat there with her mouth open in shock. Wally touched her friend's hand to indicate that she should not mention the obvious, that all the nice high school girls in town were discouraged by their parents from dating St. Michael's boys, since they were in college. "Can you tell me about it?"

Michelle was defensive in her friend's behalf. "She wasn't really dating him."

"Who?"

"Hull Jackson."

Wally relaxed a bit at hearing a familiar name. "Didn't he graduate from high school last year? He goes to St. Michael's?"

"Yes," Michelle said. "But he and Lori weren't dating. He doesn't go out with anyone seriously. He still hangs out with some of the high school kids, and that was how Lori got to know him."

"Then why did you mention him?"

"Because she really has a crush on him."

Wally thought about it. "Do you think he knew that boy, the one who was killed Wednesday night?"

Michelle shrugged. "I don't know. Can I go now, Mom?" She looked like a girl who knew she would have quite a few more questions to answer later.

"Yes." Louise turned to Wally. "We'd better make sure that the police know about this. It could mean something."

"I'll call them about it. Look, I have to be going. I'll talk to you soon." Wally hurried out to her car, wondering what it all meant.

Nate was in the kitchen when Wally came in. "Nothing," she said, reading his expression. "But there are some strange things I've been puzzled about."

"Something else strange happened," Nate said. "Renee Nichols's car was found."

"You're kidding! Where? Was it wrecked?"

"That's what is so strange. The police found it in Pennsylvania, at a rest stop on route 78. From what they said, the children's car seats were gone but the car was clean, except for a few papers, wrappers and some stickiness, probably soda, around the dashboard and steering wheel.

Otherwise it was in perfect condition. They're bringing it back to town sometime tonight."

"That's unbelievable. Do they know how long it was there?"

"Not really. But it can't have been there for long or it would have been reported. As it was, when the police checked the license plates after the car had been there over-night, they found that those had also been reported stolen, at about the same time as the car."

"Are you saying that someone was just driving it around all this time? Why didn't anyone spot it?"

Nate chuckled. "It could have been right under our noses. Who is going to wonder about one more navy blue Volvo wagon?"

"What did Renee say?"

"She told me that she didn't know whether to be happy or not. The thought of someone else driving it has her what she calls 'totally grossed out.' So I spent some time this afternoon trying to get her insurance carrier to pay for a thorough cleaning."

Wally smiled. "It was probably tidier than it was before it was stolen, considering all the children who drive around in it. Remember what used to be under the seats in my old car?" She laughed, thinking about how, after Mark's grad-uation, Nate had surprised her with a sporty no-more-carpools sedan to replace the minivan that had often felt like Wally's taxi.

Nate agreed with her, then continued. "They wouldn't pay for it, though. They would have paid the Blue Book value on the car if it had never turned up, but they won't pay to have it cleaned. Sometimes I wonder about thinking like that."

"Tell Renee that I'll clean it for her," Wally said. "I can understand her feelings. It'll be on the house."

"You're going to clean her car?" Nate asked, his eye-brows raised. "You never once cleaned your own."

"Mine was too dirty," Wally said. "And I'm not actually going to do most of the cleaning. I'll take it to the car wash, and only clean whatever they can't get. Trust me, it's good for business. Besides, I don't want Renee to feel bad. I'll do it on Sunday . . . oh, no I won't, the kids are coming. Monday morning, then. I promise."

It was surprising to see how many people showed up for Shabbat services at synagogue that evening. Sandy and Jeff Kaufman were there with their younger daughter, Felice, who looked pale and frightened. Many of their friends were also there. The rabbi made a special prayer for the return of Lori, but did not mention it in his sermon. He would save it for when she was found.

Chapter Eight

The synagogue was quite full the next morning. It was a relief that there was no bar mitzvah scheduled that day because the mood during the service was too somber. One look around at all the strained faces left no doubt that the community was under a lot of stress.

After the service, people stood around in tight knots, some speculating on what could have happened to Lori, and others offering support to the family. Wally and Nate left with the sense that everyone felt empty and helpless.

Mark's train came into the station at 1:30 and he was home by 2:00. His wavy dark brown hair had grown, and, like Wally's, curled up on the left side, just under the fake diamond earring stud that still aggravated his mother, even after all these months. "Did you have lunch yet?" she asked.

"Only once. What have you got?"

Wally made her still-growing boy a sandwich and forced herself to ask if he wanted coffee or milk with it. She was relieved when he asked for milk, and even felt a little silly for worrying that he was growing up too fast when he requested that the milk be chocolate.

As much as she hated to mention it, Wally had no choice but to tell him about Lori.

"I don't think she ran away," Mark said, after he had all the details. "She isn't the type."

"Her parents seem sure that she was kidnapped," Wally said. She explained briefly what she knew of the investigation. Then she left him to finish his lunch while she put another load of his laundry into the machine.

When he was done, Mark appeared restless. He took Sammy for a walk twice and then asked to borrow the keys to the car. Wally handed them over without a word. He seemed to want to go look for Lori. "Maybe I can help," he said.

Wally did not discourage him. As much as she wanted to hold him close, remembering the little boy he had been, she could not. He was so handsome, with his dark hair and hazel eyes, and he had the longest, thickest eyelashes in the family, which made his sisters jealous. At just over six feet tall, a lean but strong 145 pounds, mostly muscles, he was unlikely to sit still for maternal coddling. She would have to save her cuddles for little Jody.

On an impulse, Wally called Elliot and invited him to dinner the following evening. She was sure that Rachel would love to see him. She did not miss the opportunity, however, to ask if they found anything in Lori's diary, or if they had followed up on the Hull Jackson lead she had called about the day before.

"We're looking into that. Meanwhile, my partner read the entries for the last few weeks, in case whatever led up to this was mentioned. Most of it was just what she calls 'typical teenage stuff.' " Elliot paused. "But she did find a reference to a spooky stranger that we think may be worth exploring."

"What did it say?" Wally asked.

"I can't say right now," Elliot said. "But we are questioning all of Lori's friends again in reference to him, and hopefully one of them will know about this. Her mother didn't."

"What about boyfriends? Were any mentioned?"

"Hull was, recently, and several months ago she wrote that someone named Zach Greenman kept sending her poetry and then asked her out, but she refused to go. We are going to talk to him."

"Zach?"

"You know him?"

"Of course. He was in Lori's nursery school class. That was the first year I taught there."

"What else do you know about him?"

"Well, I haven't seen him in years. But I can tell you one thing. He'd never hurt Lori. He used to follow her around like a puppy."

"It's been a long time since nursery school. His hormones hadn't kicked in then. This just might be an important lead."

"But . . ." Wally broke off when she realized there was no one on the other end of the line. What had she done?

Elliot and his partner had asked many girls the same questions they were now asking Jackie Gibson in the living room of her home. He sat quietly in his chair and let Dominique do most of the talking, because she was a woman, and hopefully remembered enough about being a suburban teenager to relate to one. She had grown up in one of the towns nearby, and although she was married, she should still be able to connect with Lori's friends. Dominique probably could have continued the modeling she had done in high school and college, but she had chosen to be a police officer instead. For some reason that seemed to make most of the girls open up even more.

Dominique did not have any trouble questioning the other girls they had talked to. Their parents had all been cooperative, as were the girls, who acted a little silly, in

Elliot's opinion, but were eager to help. They seemed to
be transfixed as Dominique gestured with her long fingers
and explained the importance of their answers. But they
had not known anything. Now they were talking to Jackie
again, since she was Lori's best friend. She was their best
hope. Lori's diary specifically said that she had mentioned
to Jackie what had happened when the stranger approached
her in front of school and spoke as if he knew her.

The situation was tense though, because Jackie's mother
was stonewalling the police. She had been reluctant to let
them question her daughter, reluctant even to invite them
into her house. Finally she had, and now they were sitting
in her cramped living room on rather uncomfortable chairs.

Mrs. Gibson was a small, thin woman, very young, only
about mid-thirties, Elliot estimated. She wore tight fitting
stretch jeans, and a black sweatshirt with silver studs. On
her feet were Skecher sneakers over white slouch socks that
covered the cuffs of her jeans.

Her black hair was teased into a style that was a revival
of the sixties. Elliot believed that if a lab had to analyze a
strand of her hair, they would find that it was dyed. Her
long nails, practically talons, were painted a sort of orange-
red, with little sequins glued to the ring finger nails. She
did not really look like the mother of a teenager being
questioned about the disappearance of her best friend.
Worst of all, she was attempting to answer all the questions
herself.

"Did Lori ever say anything about a stranger?" Dominique asked Jackie.

There was a long silence. Finally Jackie seemed about
to answer. Then her mother spoke up.

"I'm sure she never mentioned any stranger," Mrs. Gibson said. She sat stiffly in the middle of a green velvet love
seat with Jackie looking very small next to her, pushed up
against the arm.

Jackie lowered her face, letting her dark, shoulder length

hair fall over it, and did not speak. She sat with her arms tight against her body, avoiding eye contact.

Elliot watched her during Dominique's questioning. He wished that he could read her mind. She looked like she had not slept in at least two days, and as if she had been crying most of that time. There were circles under her eyes, and her bare face was blotched and puffy.

Dominique's voice was soft. "Do you know anything about any boys who might be involved?"

Mrs. Gibson smiled. "That's it! That's where you should be looking. Now you understand. Why are you wasting our time?"

But Jackie just shook her head. "I don't think that's it."

"Of course that's it," Mrs. Gibson said. "Don't be so naive."

There were no explanations forthcoming, so Elliot gestured to Dominique to continue. "Does Lori have any friends who don't live in town?" she asked.

"My daughter wouldn't know about that," Mrs. Gibson said. The lines around her mouth had tightened as she set her jaw, forcing her answers out through clenched teeth. She had one hand on Jackie's knee as if to steady her, but Elliot felt that it was more to keep her from speaking.

Dominique was not one to be pushed around and she looked directly at Jackie until the girl finally shook her head. Elliot was fairly certain that her negative answer was truthful. He had not been so sure about her response, or lack of it, to the question about the stranger, and had the feeling that there was more they could have learned about him. The look in her eyes had been one of pain.

The rest of the interview was just as unproductive. Jackie could not help them as far as knowing whether Lori was upset about anything, according to her mother. The blank look on Jackie's face as her mother answered the question for her indicated to Elliot that she really did not think there was anything that was bothering Lori, to Jackie's knowledge. It would have been so simple for Jackie to answer that, as well as the other questions, and it made no sense that Mrs. Gibson would not allow it.

When they tried to insist, Mrs. Gibson threatened to call a lawyer, saying that Jackie was underage and could not be made to testify. Elliot thought it was better to just ask the questions of Mrs. Gibson for now. At least they were able to get a sense of what Jackie was thinking, since it was written all over her face. Whenever Dominique asked a question that Jackie knew the answer to, especially ones about the stranger, Jackie tensed up and lowered her eyes. She seemed to be truly afraid. At the same time, her mother squeezed her knee.

On the whole, Elliot felt that their time could have been spent better elsewhere. He just wished he knew where to look.

But as they were leaving, Elliot saw what appeared to be a graduation portrait of Jackie, with her pretty face tilted to the left, surrounded by her black hair. The picture seemed to light up a bit of the room. It was on a chrome shelf next to the door. She stared into the camera with a carefree, happy look on her face that the police officers had not seen since they walked in the door of her house.

Elliot thought back to his own senior year of high school and realized that the picture must have just been taken. It stood on the shelf all by itself. He edged closer to have a better look.

What he saw caught his eye. There were thin lines in a light layer of dust on the shelf next to the picture. He got the distinct impression that other pictures had been there, not too long ago. Perhaps they had been removed to make room for the new photo. Yet, judging by the length of the traces in the dust, he was sure that there would have been room for them as well, with just a little shuffling and re-arranging.

"Lovely picture," he said.

Mrs. Gibson came and stood between Elliot and the shelf. Although she was a small woman, about the same height as her daughter, her presence there was as forbidding as a brick wall. "Thank you. Are we done now?"

Her tone dismissed them entirely, and they said goodbye. Just in case Jackie thought of anything, Dominique handed her a business card. Elliot got the distinct impression that it would soon be part of the trash.

Out on the cold, sunny street, Dominique vented her frustration. "What's the big deal?" she asked. "Why is she being so protective of her daughter?" Elliot shrugged as they got into the patrol car. It was beyond his understanding that this woman would be so uncooperative in an investigation of the disappearance of her daughter's best friend.

"Doesn't she think that her daughter is capable of answering a few simple questions?" Dominique asked a minute later. "I'd never let my mother speak up for me!"

Elliot was thoughtful. "Unless maybe they were hiding something."

"What do you suppose that might be? Surely they didn't kidnap Lori. This isn't like the case of the mother who tried to have someone else's mother killed so she'd drop out of the competition for cheerleader."

"Mrs. Gibson might be simply trying not to get involved." Elliot's common sense told him that was most likely the reason for the stonewalling. "Maybe she's worried that something could happen to Jackie if they answer questions. I personally can't understand that kind of thinking, but we may have to find another way to find out what they're trying to conceal. And I'm sure Mrs. Gibson isn't the one to ask."

"We need a lead," Dominique said, as she pulled the car out into road, steering carefully past a line of parked cars on the crowded street. "And we need the whole truth, not like what we got from Mrs. Gibson. It's time to go after the boys."

They found Hull Jackson's house not far from where Jackie and her parents lived. He was home, apparently waiting for them. They were relieved, because when they had called earlier, his mother had said he was out, and she didn't know when he would return.

Hull shook hands with them politely, his friendly blue eyes only mildly concerned by their presence. Despite the cold November day, he was dressed in a dark t-shirt with rolled sleeves that displayed the fact that he lifted weights, and it was tucked neatly into his ironed jeans. When he invited them inside to talk, his mother bustled around offering them coffee or tea and home-baked cookies. It was easy to see where Hull got his manners and looks. His mother had the same color eyes and jet black hair that her son had.

"How can my son help you?" Mrs. Jackson asked. Elliot was afraid that they were up against another mother who spoke for her child, and he shuddered.

"Mom," Hull said. "I can talk for myself.' He turned to the officers. "What can I do for you?"

"I'm sure that you heard about Lori Kaufman's disappearance," Elliot said. Remembering Mrs. Morris's contention that there was some relationship to it, he added, "And Brian Lambert's murder."

Mrs. Jackson paled considerably, but remained silent.

"Yes," Hull said. "I heard. It's terrible. So sad."

"We are investigating," Elliot said. "We hoped that maybe you could tell us something that would help us find Lori, or maybe who killed Brian."

Hull's face was blank. "I don't think so."

"Did you know Brian?"

"Yes. I think he was in English with me. I remember that he was missing the day before yesterday. And right after class people were talking about it."

"Did you hear anything that could help?"

"No."

Dominique shifted uneasily in her chair. "Did he know Lori?"

"I don't think so. Lori never came to the campus and I don't remember Brian hanging out with me and Lori in town."

Dominique moved closer to the edge of her seat. "So you hung around with Lori?"

"She was in the group."

"What group?"

"The seniors from high school."

"And you hung out with them? But you're in college now."

"Yes. I haven't made any friends though, because I live at home." He seemed very sad.

"I tell him to stay on campus more," his mother said. "But he just wants to come home. He's so quiet and shy."

Elliot wondered why Lori was attracted to that type, but Hull's looks left little room to speculate. He was very handsome, if a little on the not-too-bright side. St. Michael's had a great basketball team but they weren't known for their scholars, except in some of the professional programs.

"I guess I can't really help you," Hull said.

"Will you call us if you think of anything?"

"Okay." He shook their hands and watched as they got into the police car, and he was still standing on the porch as they turned the corner.

"I don't think he knows anything," Elliot said.

"Why not?"

"He just seems so simple and straightforward."

"True. But it could be an act."

"We'll see." Elliot looked at the address for the Greenman kid. It was in the most upscale section of town. He turned the ignition key and headed the car up the hill toward the Greenmans'.

"I suppose that lady, what's her name, Morris, is going

to call you again and want more information," Dominique said.

"Actually I'm having dinner at her house tomorrow."

"Do you think that's right?"

"I'm not going to tell her anything. I admit she's kind of a pest, but I'd like to see her daughter again. Rachel and I were buddies in high school."

"So that's why you're going. I knew there must be a reason. Is she still single?"

"No. She's married with a kid."

"Then I don't understand."

"She's very nice and I'd like to see her."

"Just make sure her mother doesn't pump you too much."

"That's it," Dominique said a few minutes later. "The third house in." They drove up to the highest point in the town, past several very large homes with expansive front lawns and views of Manhattan. Dominique readied herself by turning the page in her notebook. As soon as the car came to a stop, she was out the door. "Let me ask the questions."

"Suit yourself."

Zachary Greenman's mother stood in the doorway perfectly dressed, with perfect blow-dried hair and more jewelry than most people wore, especially with running suits. Hers was expensive, brightly colored, with big patches of multi-patterned fabric offset by gold trim, and her sneakers looked as if they just came out of the box. She looked at her watch. "I expected you a half-hour ago. I have an appointment."

"We are here to talk to Zach," Dominique said. "It's okay with us if you have to leave."

"Well it isn't okay with me, Miss. I will be present when you question him. Perhaps I should call my lawyer?"

"That won't be necessary, Mrs. Greenman," Elliot said,

forcing a smile to his lips. "We are asking several people background questions regarding Lori's disappearance. That's all we are going to ask Zach."

"My husband would have a few things to say about this if he were home," Mrs. Greenman said. "But he is away on business. And I have things to do. Can we please hurry?"

"Yes, ma'am. Where is Zachary?"

"Oh, yes. I almost forgot. Zach, darling," she called, in a syrupy sing-song, "Please come down here."

Large, untied, dirty tennis shoes were soon followed down the steps by the pimply teenager who wore them. His kinky brown hair was tied back in a pony tail, exposing largish ears, and he wore a tie dye shirt that looked as if it could have originated in the '60s. He barely looked at the officers, or his mother. "Can we get this over with? I have things to do."

"Zachary, don't be rude. These officers are just trying to help that poor girl. You want to help her too, don't you?"

For the first time since they entered the house, Elliot had the sensation that someone was being genuine. Zachary had a look of intense longing on his face when he responded, "Yes! I'll do anything to help."

"May we sit down?" Dominique asked.

Mrs. Greenman looked disgusted but led them over to an upholstered bench that lined one of the walls in the hallway. Her manner was in such contrast to Mrs. Jackson's that Elliot saw Dominique curl her lip. Mrs. Greenman stood next to Zach, who sat nervously on the edge of the bench next to Dominique. Elliot was left to stand, and found himself looking around at the magnificently decorated house, and up the wide staircase to the floor above. He couldn't help wondering if, should they find it necessary to go to Zach's room, it would be as neat as the rest of the house. Somehow he doubted it.

"You were interested in dating Lori at one time, weren't

you?" Dominique asked, after a series of preliminary questions.

Zach's eyes lowered. "Yes."

"But she turned you down?"

"Yes."

"I told Zachie that it was no big deal," Mrs. Greenman said. "What's so special about Lori Kaufman anyway? You've been mooning over her for years and she never even talked to you. I would have thought you'd be over her by now."

"You don't understand."

Elliot felt that was an understatement. He was willing to bet that Mrs. Greenman didn't understand her son at all. The boy was obviously still in love with Lori, and his mother was clueless. Maybe he did have something to do with her disappearance. He looked guilty enough.

"When was the last time you saw Lori?" Dominique asked.

"Wednesday at school."

"What time?"

"Two-thirty."

"And not after that?"

"No. I heard she vanished that night, but I was home studying, so I didn't see her."

"Can you verify that, Mrs. Greenman?" Dominique asked.

"Uh, no."

"You don't know if he was home?"

"I'm sure he was if he says so. I was still at work."

"Until when?"

"Eight. And it takes over an hour to get home, so I would say I didn't see Zach before nine-thirty."

"You saw him then?"

Mrs. Greenman seemed to ponder that. "I'm not sure. I don't really remember."

"You didn't see him as soon as you got home?" Dominique asked.

"Officer, this is not a case for the Department of Youth and Family Services. I'm a busy woman and I work hard. I'm sure I must have seen him at some point."

"What about your husband?"

"What about him?"

"Was he here that night?"

"No. I told you. He is out of town."

Elliot was becoming impatient. "Was he out of town that night?"

Mrs. Greenman stared at him blankly. "Yes. Didn't I just say that?"

Dominique cleared her throat. "Is there anyone else living here who might have seen Zach and could verify his story?"

"No. His sister is away at school."

Dominique put her hand on Zach's. "Did anyone call, someone who might remember the time and that you were here?"

"I don't get many calls, and everyone knows my parents are never home," he said, with a trace of bitterness.

His mother seemed oblivious to the tone of his voice, and just jiggled her car keys. "I really must leave," she said. "I'll be late otherwise."

"Go ahead, Mom," Zach said. "I'll be fine."

"Thank you, sweetheart. There's a microwave dinner in the freezer." She blew a kiss at the air over Zach's head. "Bye."

"As usual," he said, as the door to the garage slammed. They all sat without speaking while the electric door opened, the car pulled out, and the door closed again.

"You're alone a lot, aren't you?" Dominique asked. "That's why you don't have anyone to speak up for you."

"I suppose. But I had nothing to do with Lori's disappearance. I'm trying to . . . uh, I, didn't do it. That's all I have to say on the subject." He clammed up and it was clear they would get nothing out of him.

"We may be back with more questions," Elliot said. He had serious concerns about the kid, and felt there was a distinct possibility that he knew more than he had said.

Dominique felt the same way, and she told Elliot this in the car on the way back to the station. And when she pulled into the numbered parking space at the precinct, she shook her head. "If he did kidnap her, I don't want to think of where she is now."

Elliot nodded. "We'd better assign people to watch him. Just in case."

Chapter Nine

Jody, Rachel, and her carrot-topped husband, Adam, the source of the baby's red hair, arrived in the middle of a downpour that had started at dawn. Although they were due at noon, the traffic had been so awful that it took them until 1:00 to finally get to Grosvenor. Debbie and her drenched laundry rolled in at around 2:00.

Wally got to play with the soft, sweet-smelling baby for only a short time before Grandpa Nate and Uncle Mark took over. Debbie and Rachel helped in the kitchen, gossiping about their old friends and Debbie's occasional boyfriends, none of whom seemed to be the right one for her.

It made Wally happy, watching her daughters like this. They had never gotten along so well; in fact, they had fought almost constantly until the day that Rachel went away to college. Then, as if by magic, she and Debbie had found the good relationship they now shared.

Rachel had Wally's coloring: dark brown hair and brown eyes. She was under five feet tall, like Wally, with long hair, which, since the baby arrived, was pulled back in a ponytail. She looked even younger than Debbie most of the time.

Debbie was also petite, almost as short as Rachel, but she had light brown hair that was usually blond, thanks to the hairdresser. With her blue-green eyes, the same as Nate's, she looked sensational and sophisticated, even in jeans. Her priorities at this point in her life were very different from Rachel's, but they still got along. After all the years of fighting, it was a relief.

Elliot arrived at 4:00. He and Rachel spent a half hour in the den remembering high school and looking at the baby. Elliot was still single, and Wally hoped he would find someone soon. He was such a nice young man.

Debbie seemed to be drawn to the conversation in the den, leaving Wally to wonder if they had friends in common. She could not remember any, yet Debbie kept going into the room where Rachel and Elliot chatted, almost like a little sister watching a big sister with a beau. It puzzled Wally, but she reasoned that maybe Debbie was just looking for some clues about what to expect from law school. Elliot was in his third year of law school, studying at night, well ahead of Debbie, who was in her third month.

Just before 5:00 they sat down to dinner. Wally asked Elliot about the house he was buying from his parents, now that they had moved to Florida.

"It's fine, I guess," Elliot said. "I find myself taking care of it the way my father used to when I thought he was just being obsessive."

"Do you think your parents will move back up here?" Rachel asked.

"They seem to love Florida," Elliot said. "Even during the hot sticky summer. My father plays golf or tennis every day and then they sit by the pool. Meanwhile, I have to rake the leaves and shovel snow just like I did when I was a kid."

They had fallen into easy conversation. Adam and Rachel started talking about the houses they were looking at in Westchester. Wally wanted them to move closer to home, but did not say a word. That was for them to decide.

As Nate cut the roast beef, Wally brought the case up again. "Did anyone know anything about the strange man Lori mentioned in her diary?" she asked.

Elliot passed his plate for some of the rosemary roasted potatoes. "I'm not supposed to talk about this, Mrs. Morris."

Wally was really disappointed. She had been hoping to find out what was going on. Now she could not. As she was wondering what she could say to change his mind, her eyes fell on Debbie, who was staring intensely at Elliot.

"Please? It's so important," Debbie asked him.

He wiped his lips with his napkin and sighed. But he seemed unable to refuse to answer Debbie. "No one remembered anything. I think Jackie might have, but it was hard to find out anything from her."

Mark snorted. "She's always been closed-mouthed. She never talked about herself. Most people would think that was shyness, but she seemed really secretive to me."

"Mrs. Gibson didn't let her say anything at all," Elliot said. "Maybe she didn't realize how important this is, or maybe she just didn't want to get involved. When I mentioned the stranger, she said Jackie didn't know a thing about it. And Jackie didn't disagree with her, at least not verbally." He paused.

"And then Mrs. Gibson asked us to leave. She said it was obvious that they couldn't help me."

"You would think they'd do anything to help," Debbie said, staring at Elliot. "Lori is her best friend, isn't she?"

He nodded back, keeping eye contact a moment longer than necessary. Wally looked at Nate in surprise, and could tell by his face that he had seen it too.

"What about the two boys Lori wrote about in her diary?" Wally asked. "Zach Greenman and Hull Jackson?"

Mark put down his fork. "Who? Did you say Hull Jackson?"

"Yes," Elliot said. "Do you know him?"

"I did. He went to high school with me."

"What can you tell me about him?"

"Nothing much. He's quiet. I sometimes think it's because he doesn't quite get what's going on."

"Mark!"

"Sorry, Mom. I know I shouldn't say nasty things about people. But it's true."

"Do you think he had anything to do with Lori's disappearance?" Elliot asked.

"No. I wouldn't think so. I could call him and talk to him later, and maybe feel him out about it."

"It might be worth a try," Elliot said. "See what you can find out. It's possible that he saw someone else but didn't put it together."

"Okay."

Wally was satisfied. "Anyone for dessert?"

Elliot stayed long after dinner, talking with the family, but as Rachel and her husband packed up to leave he said goodbye. Although Debbie was still doing her laundry, she stopped long enough to say goodbye to all of them. She seemed to linger near Elliot.

By the time the laundry was done and folded, Nate had decided to take Debbie back to her apartment in the city. He did not want her traveling alone at night.

Wally felt a sense of emptiness when they were all gone. She hated that feeling, and it reminded her of how all the neighborhood children drifted away after her grandmother died, driven off by her mother's desolation. It still hurt. Fortunately, Mark was still there, although only until Tuesday morning, and then the house would be too quiet again.

But the day had been lovely. She thought about it while she finished putting away the dinner dishes, and about her younger daughter's strange behavior, almost as if she had a schoolgirl crush on Elliot. Worse things could happen.

Eventually her mind drifted back to Lori. It seemed to be the only thing she could think about. And what really frustrated her was that thinking was about all she could do to help.

Chapter Ten

Early Monday morning, after only one cup of coffee, Wally picked up Renee Nichols's blue Volvo station wagon from in front of her gray Cape Cod-style house and drove it to the car wash. The still-groggy attendants cleaned some wrappers and an old local weekly newspaper out of it and vacuumed it halfheartedly. Yawning in sympathy, Wally made them do it a second time, more carefully, since she did not want to have to put her own hands down between the seats. She wondered how the police who found the car could consider it clean, when there was so much hidden yuck.

Something got caught in the vacuum hose. The attendant stopped the suction, reached deep down into the space between the bottom and back of one of the seats and withdrew his hand, full of what appeared to be trash. He threw several broken crayons into the refuse barrel and pried a sticky, fuzzy lollipop off his hand with a grimace. Then he handed Wally a pen.

It was a silver Parker pen, expensive, if Wally correctly remembered the last time she priced that kind of thing, and she was sure that Renee would be happy to see it again. It had probably been lost for months. She went over to the telephone to give her the good news while the car was working its way through the suds.

Renee picked up the phone on the third ring, sounding out of breath when she said hello.

"Good news," Wally said, enthusiastically, after she told Renee who she was. "I found your pen."

Her information was not met with the response that she expected. "My pen?"

"Your silver pen," Wally said. "It was way down in the seats. It must have been missing for a while."

"I don't have a silver pen," Renee said. "I'm lucky if I have a Bic. Usually it's just pencils and crayons around here."

"Oh." Wally began to wish she had not called and hoped she could hang up soon. Maybe her judgment had been clouded by the lack of caffeine. She wasn't sure. In any case, this was embarrassing and she felt deflated. "Well, maybe it belonged to a friend of yours. I'll show it to you when I bring your car. You might recognize it. The car shouldn't be much longer," she added, wondering if she had time while it passed through the suds to get a quick cup of coffee from the car wash's hospitality center, "and I'll bring it right back."

Renee's voice sounded sort of tentative. "Okay." There was a lot of childish noise in the background as she hung up.

Styrofoam cup in hand, Wally paid the thirteen dollars plus tax at the cashier and walked outside. There she generously tipped the attendants at the exit of the car wash and explained that she wanted them to really clean out the inside of the car, not only the windows and dashboard, but all the surfaces. The carpet was in good shape, so she didn't worry too much about it, but she had noticed when she drove over there that everything was kind of sticky inside.

She suspected that it had always been that way, at least while it was in Renee's possession, but she had them clean it anyway, with extra elbow grease. At the last minute she had them spray a quarter of a can of "eau de new car" air freshener into the interior.

The car was sparkling when she presented it to Renee. Wally took all the credit, and even though she had not actually done any of the work, she had paid a lot to have the job done, after all. It made her feel good to take care of her husband's client and the look of relief on Renee's face was enough to make the extra money worth it.

Renee got in and settled into the driver's seat. She sniffed the new car smell and looked all around, then checked the ashtrays and opened the glove compartment, which Wally had tidied while she waited at a stop light.

Puzzled, Renee reached in and pulled something out. "What are these?" In her hand she held some tapes.

"Aren't they yours?" Wally asked.

"No," she replied with a grimace. "Great. I just realized that not only are the two child safety seats gone, all the *Barney* and *Sesame Street* tapes are missing. I'll have to replace them, even if they make my brain fry."

"What are those tapes, then?" Wally asked, pointing at the open glove compartment.

"Let's see." Renee went through them, tossing each one onto the seat next to her as she read the title. "*Peter and the Wolf, The Nutcracker*, something about animals, and *Peter, Paul and Mommy*. My kids have never heard this stuff. Maybe it would be good for them. But isn't it strange?" Renee got out of the car and bent to pick her crying baby up from her stroller.

Wally had to agree. They were just the kind of things that her own children had listened to. She figured that the thing about animals was Camille St. Saens' *Carnival of the Animals*.

Just before she left, Wally remembered the pen. She

pulled it out of her purse and held it up for Renee to see.

"Nope," the young woman said, balancing a Similac-stained baby on her hip, and holding a hand-me-down–wearing toddler by the hand to keep him from running into the street. Wally was glad that Renee's older two were in their car pool on the way to nursery school, or they would have distracted their mother even more. "I've never seen it before," Renee added decisively.

"Do you want to keep it and ask your friends?" Wally asked.

"It would be lost in two minutes," Renee said. "You hang onto it. I promise I'll ask everyone who has ever been in my car."

Wally felt uncomfortable about it, but agreed. She put it back in her purse and said goodbye to Renee before getting into her own car and hurrying to the nursery school.

It was a morning filled with turkeys, in celebration of the upcoming holiday. Wally taught the children a song about the pilgrims, and the children walked around the room pretending to gobble like turkeys. After juice and crackers, the children worked on their turkey decorations, which involved glue, blunt scissors, and patience.

At five minutes to eleven, the nursery school director signaled Wally to come out into the hall. Puzzled, she stepped out of the classroom.

"Please go to the office," the director said. "I'll watch your class."

Wally hurried down to the office, wondering why she had been summoned. But when she got there she understood. Timmy's mother was standing there, very pale.

"He might try to take Timmy," she explained, referring to her ex-husband. "You have to protect him." She took a paper out of her purse. "This is a court order. I have full custody. My ex has no visitation at all."

Wally did not know what to say, or why Timmy's mother felt she had to tell her about this. She already knew that the parents were divorced and she was doing everything she could to help Timmy.

"You have to promise me that if he ever finds out where Timmy is, you'll tell me. I have to protect him."

"Of course," Wally said, hoping that the chills which ran down her neck wouldn't cause her to shiver openly. She hated situations like this.

Timmy's mother looked relieved. "Thanks." She turned to go, and then stopped, looking back at Wally and smiling through tears. "I guess I'll be on time to pick him up today."

On her way home, Wally stopped at the bakery near the high school to get Mark one of his favorite treats. As she went back to her car, she heard a voice. Turning, she saw someone wave. She waited for the two girls, about fifteen years old, to come over to her. One of them, tall with dark hair, looked familiar, and Wally tried to remember her name.

"Hi," the girl said. She waited expectantly.

Wally struggled to remember the girl's name, but could not. So many children, from just over the age of five up to one year younger than Mark, the first class that Wally taught in nursery school, came to say "hi" to her. She usually knew their names, but not this time.

The girl looked hurt.

"I'm sorry," Wally apologized. "I'm sure I'd remember if you just told me your name."

"Emily Morgan."

A mental snapshot of a little blond girl with pigtails jumped into Wally's mind. "Emily? You're so grown up!"

Emily beamed at Wally, and turned to her friend. "Wally was my teacher when I was four." Turning back to Wally, she introduced her friend. "I just wanted to say hello," Emily concluded. "It's so nice to see you."

Wally watched as the girls went into a pizza shop. Emily

didn't look anything like she did as a child. Her long hair, which had been blond, had turned very dark, nearly black, more like her mother's, as Wally remembered. That happened to so many of the girls. It may have even happened to Debbie, Wally realized, although she had not seen Debbie's hair "au natural" in years.

When she arrived home, Wally stopped at Nate's office before going into the house. Mary Jane, the intern Nate was currently training in the insurance part of his business, smiled as Wally walked in.

Nate was showing her how to compute car insurance rates. Wally took off her jacket and put it on the coat rack, then sat down to wait for her husband.

The phone rang and Wally grabbed it, so as not to let it interrupt the lesson. After she wrote down the message for Nate, she went into his office to put it on his desk. It was in one of the double stalls of the old barn, his inner sanctum where he met with special insurance customers in private. Another double stall was used for the investment business he ran and was where he wrote his newsletter. The people who had routine insurance matters to handle just sat at Mary Jane's desk in one of the wooden captain's chairs.

"Sorry to keep you waiting," Nate said, as Wally came out of his office. "Did you want something?"

"A kiss would be nice," Wally said, putting her jacket back on and handing Nate his. "I got Renee's car washed, as promised."

"Thanks. I'm sure she appreciated it." He held the door open for her, and she went outside.

Her face must have given her away, though, because Nate put his hand on her arm, stopping her. "Is something wrong?"

"Not exactly. There was, uh, extra stuff in the car."

"A bonus?"

"I guess. Whatever." Wally decided to put it out of her

mind. It was such a lovely autumn day that it seemed a shame to go into the house.

Mary Jane came hurrying down the driveway after them, her coat half on, juggling her college textbooks. "I'm off. The machine is on. See you tomorrow."

Nate stood watching her get into her car as Wally pushed the kitchen door open. Mark, still dressed in the sweats he wore to bed, was in the kitchen when they arrived.

"I talked to Hull."

Nate, closing the door behind himself, raised his eyebrows. "And?"

"Nothing," Mark said, shaking his head. "I don't think he particularly noticed Lori. I got the sense that he was just doing his best to try to keep up with the group."

Wally knew other kids like that. With some of them it was obvious from early childhood that they would always be out of the loop. "That's sad."

"Yeah. By the way, I was thinking about the other kid, Zach. I remembered that I know him too. He's a computer geek. Very good at it."

"Could you call him and try to find out something?"

"I don't think so. He'd know in an instant why I was calling. Not like Hull."

"Do you know him well enough to know if he might have had anything to do with Lori's disappearance?"

"No. He really kept to himself last year. He was in my math class though." Mark tapped his head. "A real genius."

Wally remembered that Zach was very bright when he was younger, too. He could read and do fairly advanced math when he was four. With even more to think about, she made a quick lunch and checked the household mail. There were no messages on the machine, no word on Lori. She wished there was something she could do.

Elliot and Dominique spent the day at the high school asking Lori's classmates if they had seen anything. Since he was a graduate, Dominique had let Elliot lead the way around the school to question everyone, and then to the gym so that they could ask the cheerleading coach about the specifics of last Wednesday night. Then, they again followed the most likely route that Lori would have taken to go home, searching for clues starting from the point where she left the school. But for the most part they came up empty, and Elliot felt that they were just repeating themselves for no gain.

They had come tantalizingly close to one lead. One girl, when asked about strangers, said that she saw someone hanging around outside the school entrance that Lori used, on several days right before Lori disappeared. When they asked about the man, she was unable to give any kind of description, except to say that he looked like he could be someone's father. That was her answer to "how old was the man?" "What kind of car was he driving?" was answered by "a regular car, you know the usual kind." She could give no further description. It was terribly frustrating.

"What do you suppose she meant by a 'regular car'?" Elliot asked. "I can't believe that a suburban teen doesn't know what kind of car is what."

"I'm not sure what she means," Dominique said. "Probably one that a lot of people have. Maybe a wagon, an SUV, or a minivan."

"We could try to show her pictures of some, and see if she recognizes any."

"Maybe we'll do that. At least it's something."

There was no information that would help with the investigations of either of the boys, other than some love poems in Zach Greenman's locker that were addressed to Lori. Frustrated, Elliot let Dominique drive. More than anything, he wanted to solve this case, and solve it quickly. It would not only increase the chances that Lori would still be alive, but also show that they, Elliot Levine and Dominique Scott, could do it. That would be a nice addition to their record. And it would keep Jaeger off their backs.

"Don't worry so much about Jaeger," Elliot advised his partner. "He just likes to give you a hard time. Besides, he's still furious that they won't let us tag along on the murder case."

"True." Dominique said with a laugh. "He likes to give you a hard time too, you know."

"Right. But we are going to solve this case and make him eat his criticisms." That was easy and brave to say, Elliot thought, but so far they had very little to go on. Lori Kaufman was last seen at a cheerleading practice on Wednesday of the previous week. No one had seen her since she started walking home. And on top of that, a murder had been committed, possibly at the same time and in the same vicinity as the disappearance. And two teenage boys might or might not be involved. That was the sum total of what they had.

Dominique sighed. Elliot understood.

Chapter Eleven

Wally had not heard from Elliot in two days, and Nate was against her pestering him. He seemed to think (incorrectly, Wally thought) that she was annoying the police and holding up their investigation. But how could she stay out of it? The whole town was buzzing, and the general speculation on Lori's well-being was negative.

There had been two serious scares: the bodies of two girls had been found dead alongside highways, one on Long Beach Island and the other out of state. Either one could have been Lori, based on the general description the police were using. The first was identified as someone else soon after, but the other was so close that Jeff Kaufman was taken to Connecticut to see if he could identify her. The body was not Lori's, but the experience proved devastating.

Sandy and Jeff were being treated as mourners, and several of the high school seniors were planning what sounded suspiciously like a memorial.

But as Wally had lunch, alone, since Nate was in New York City at a seminar, she could not give up the hope that

Lori would be found alive and only slightly shaken. She shook her head at that notion, however, realizing that at the very least, Lori would be severely traumatized.

There were many things to do but somehow she could not start them, or even think about starting them. For the last two nights she had lain awake for hours remembering all the things she was supposed to have done during the day, which by then it was too late to do. There was nothing much she could accomplish at midnight.

After lunch, Wally forced herself to stay seated until she had a plan. Taking a pad and a pen, she started a list of all the things that had to be done. There was one section for things that she would have to buy for Thanksgiving, one for errands, and one for phone calls that she had to make.

She surveyed the list. Since each part would keep her busy for hours, except for the phone section, she reached for the receiver to make the first call.

But just as she did so, the phone rang. It was Elliot.

"How are you, Mrs. Morris?" he said, as politely as ever.

"Fine. Have you found her yet?"

"No. And I just checked with the people on the murder case. The information they gave me is public, so I can tell you this much. Other than identifying the weapon as a hunting knife, they have no leads. They found some smudges and think it's possible that the murderer may have put his hands into Brian's blood, but they don't know where he may have put them afterward, and they can't get any fingerprints."

"That's too bad. I suppose that the Kaufmans are beside themselves."

"They are, particularly after the two scares," Elliot said. "I wish I had better news. But I wanted to thank you for dinner the other night. Your family was wonderful to include me."

"They enjoyed seeing you," Wally said. "Rachel was very happy that you came."

"Did Debbie get home all right?" Elliot said. "She had all that laundry and all."

Wally smiled. That question was a good sign. "Her father took her home. Thank you for asking."

"Uh, well," Elliot said, sputtering, "I'll call you if anything comes up."

"Elliot? Tell me your gut feeling. Do you think it was one of the boys?"

"Maybe Zach. He hasn't been going to school. We've had someone watching him and he hasn't left his house at all."

"Then why would you think he took her? Wouldn't he have to go out to, I don't know, feed her, or something?"

The line was silent. "If she needed food," Elliot said quietly.

"Oh! You can't think she's . . ."

"I really don't know. Nothing makes sense so far."

"Are you going to arrest Zach?"

"Maybe. You mustn't say anything about this. I shouldn't have told you."

"I won't. Call me if you have anything else, though, won't you?"

"I could get into trouble."

"I understand."

"I'll see what I can do," Elliot said.

"Thank you." Wally hung up, and fought off the urge to call Debbie and tell her that Elliot was interested. She tried never to meddle. Within reason, of course. Let them work it out for themselves, she thought, if that was what they wanted to do.

But she knew that if she stayed home, she would make that call. She picked up her jacket and left.

Zach Greenman kept going around in her head. It just didn't seem possible that he did it. Wally knew that Nate would say that she was protecting her own as usual, refusing to believe that a former student of hers could do something bad. He had chastised her for that before. But Wally felt that she had to do something, and maybe this would help.

She checked the phone directory in her car and drove over to the Greenman house, past some of the nicest houses in Grosvenor. Several of them sported banners with turkeys on them, reminding Wally again of the upcoming Thanksgiving celebration. But who in this town could possibly be in the mood to celebrate if Lori wasn't returned by then?

Finally she found the Greenman home. It truly was beautiful, and Wally was impressed as she walked up the path past the columns and rang the doorbell. For several minutes it seemed that no one was home, but finally Zach, who looked even grungier than the other high school kids she had seen lately, opened the door. He blinked, as if the watery autumn sunlight was too bright. "Yes?"

"Zach," Wally said. "You probably don't remember me, but I was your nursery school teacher."

Zach looked at her suspiciously. While Wally was aware that many of the children she taught forgot her, she felt it reasonable for them to remember when they were reminded. After all, she liked to think she hadn't changed all that much since then.

"Mrs. Morris?"

"You remember?"

"Yes," he said, looking anything but happy to see her. "What do you want?"

"I came to find out . . ." She stopped, unable to think of how to finish that sentence. She tried a new approach. "You couldn't possibly have had anything to do with Lori Kaufman's disappearance."

Zach nodded. "I didn't."

"I didn't think so. But you haven't been to school and the police might get the wrong idea."

"How can I go to school when she's missing?"

"You love her that much?"

"No, well, yes, but that isn't it." He seemed exasperated.

Wally gently touched his shoulder. He wasn't that tall, only about 5'6", and he seemed younger than a high school senior. "Do you think you can explain it to me? Maybe I can help."

"You wouldn't understand. My parents don't. But they don't know I've been staying home. I called the school and said I was my Dad and that I had the flu."

"They didn't believe that, did they?"

"I guess so. They didn't call my parents at work."

Wally thought that might be true. Elliot knew that Zach was out of school, but he didn't say that he was truant. She forced an encouraging smile, glad that her children were past that age, and also that she and Nate had always been home during the day, so they couldn't do things like cut school. Not that her fine, upstanding children ever would.

"May I come in, so we can talk?"

"My parents wouldn't like that."

"I understand completely," Wally said, but she made no move to leave.

Zach seemed to change his mind, or maybe he just wanted to talk to someone. "I guess it would be okay."

Wally followed him through the main foyer, past the living room. From what she could see it was done in a decorator style, without the little additions of family personality to take the cold sterility out of it. Still, it was attractive, if Wally wanted to be honest with herself.

Zach led the way into the kitchen, where the remains of breakfast were in and around the sink. "I have been trying to find her."

"How?"

"On the internet. I sent around a picture, nationwide, with a bio. I have to be here to see if anyone responds."

"Why didn't you tell that to the police?"

"I can't. There is supposed to be a blackout on news of her disappearance. I thought I'd get in trouble."

"You might find that you'd get out of more trouble than you'd get into," Wally cautioned.

"You mean they think that I took her away?"

"They might."

"But how can I tell them I violated the blackout?"

"Do you have any proof that you've been searching for her?"

"I can print out a copy of the electronic poster I put on the bulletin board."

"That might help. And I could say that it was here when I came, so that you didn't just put it on after I warned you that you might be a suspect."

Zach got very pale, and Wally was sorry that she had been so blunt. "Okay," the boy said. "But there would be other ways to prove that it's been on the board since I found out she was missing."

"Forgive my computer illiteracy. You always were very bright."

The look that Zach gave Wally told her that one didn't have to be a rocket scientist to know that much about computers, but she forgave him, what with the stress and all. Then she called Elliot's office and filled him in on the situation. He sounded unconvinced and very annoyed at first, even implying that just because someone had her as a nursery school teacher didn't guarantee that his life would be full of roses. But she kept at him until he promised to come right over to Zach's and get a statement. Wally smiled another encouraging smile at the boy, wishing his mother was there for him, and left.

It had been almost six full days since Lori disappeared, and, although Wally knew that several people were providing dinners for the Kaufmans, she worried that they might need some basics. So she drove over to see if she could get them anything.

Sandy seemed glad to see her. "Please come in," she said. "But we haven't heard anything."

"I know," Wally said. "I'm sorry. I just came to see if I could get you anything at the grocery store. Milk, cereal, fruit, whatever."

"Oh, thank you!" Sandy gushed. "I really do need to go, but I can't bear to see everyone. I was planning to drive to another county to shop anonymously."

"Never mind that," Wally said. "Just give me a list." She fished through her pocketbook for a pen and the little notepad she always carried with her.

Sandy was ahead of her as they went into the kitchen. She opened the fridge and started to call out items. "Milk, orange juice, eggs, cottage cheese, fruit, and margarine." When she was done in there, she turned and headed for the pantry. "This is so nice of you," she said. "I don't . . ." She stopped speaking suddenly, and Wally watched in amazement as Sandy's eyes widened, her mouth opened, and she burst into tears.

Loud, wracking sobs filled the room. Jeff came in from the den, looked at Wally, and then at his wife. "Oh, no . . ." He put his arm around her as she sank down into a kitchen chair.

Wally was speechless. She had no idea what to do or why this was happening. She stood as still as she could and waited.

Sandy stopped crying, and, gasping for air, craned her head to look at her husband. "No, Jeff. I didn't hear anything. I'm sorry I scared you. It's just that," she paused, desperately trying to catch her breath, "Wally has the same pen as Lori."

She turned her embarrassed face to Wally. "I'm so sorry. I didn't mean to react that way. It was silly and childish. But your pen is just like the one she loved so much. It was a bat mitzvah present. Lori always had the Parker with her."

Wally stared down at the pen in her hand. It was not her

usual pen. It was the one that she found when she cleaned out Renee Nichols's car. Without thinking, she handed it to Sandy.

Sandy looked at it halfheartedly. But then she inspected it closely. "Look!" She pointed at the bottom. "It's crushed a little, just like Lori's. Remember, Jeff? She caught it in the car door when she was getting out one day. You tried to fix it."

Jeff took the pen from his wife. "This is Lori's pen! I can see the scratches I made when I was straightening it." He turned to Wally. "How did you get it?"

"I found it in a car, one that had been stolen, when I was cleaning it for the owner." She was finally able to think again. "Let me call Elliot Levine right away."

She dialed the number quickly, hoping that he was back from the Greenmans'. When he answered, she explained what had happened.

"Does this clear both the boys?" Wally asked quietly, so that Sandy would not overhear.

"We can't be sure."

"But neither of them could have driven to Pennsylvania. Oh, forget it. Just come and check out this pen."

"Can you call Mrs. Nichols?" Elliot asked. "We'll want to go over that car."

Wally promised she would, and said she would wait for him at the Kaufmans'. Then they could go to see Mrs. Nichols together. She also promised Sandy that she'd get the shopping done somehow.

Elliot and his partner arrived just a few minutes later. They examined the pen and listened to the Kaufmans' assurances that it was definitely Lori's and that she usually had it with her. They promised to let the Kaufmans know what this new lead would turn up. Then they took Wally with them to examine Renee Nichols's Volvo.

Chapter Twelve

"I hate to break this to you, Mrs. Nichols," Elliot said, after they explained the situation to her. "But we are going to have to take your car in so we can go over it. Considering the fact that it was missing until just after the kidnapping, and that Lori's pen was found in it, I think it is conceivable that the kidnapper used this vehicle."

Renee nodded grimly. "When can I have it back?"

"As soon as possible," Dominique replied.

"I'm supposed to drive the soccer car pool today," Renee said. "But I'll rearrange it. You have to take the car. Maybe it'll help."

"Thanks for understanding, ma'am," Elliot said. "We'll hurry." He started to fill out the paperwork.

"We have a few questions, Mrs. Nichols," Dominique said. "Is the car in the same condition as when it was returned?"

"What do you mean?"

"Is this the way it was when it was found?"

"Oh, no," Renee said. "Wally cleaned it out for me. That was how she found that pen."

All their eyes turned toward Wally and she suddenly felt very warm. She tugged at the left side of her hair self-consciously and waited.

"How well did you clean it, Mrs. Morris?" Elliot asked.

"Um," she said, guilt washing over her. "I didn't know . . . I cleaned it thoroughly, so that Renee would feel better."

"Maybe you'd better come to the station with us," Elliot's partner said. "We'll want to get a list of everything that was in the car."

Wally couldn't shake her feeling of having made a major blunder. How could she face Sandy and Jeff if she had destroyed evidence that might have led to Lori? What if she were held up for a long time at the police station and couldn't help Sandy out after all? Miserable, she asked if she could first call her friend Louise to arrange for her to do Sandy's shopping.

Then it was time to go to the police station. They put Wally into a small room and had her list all the things she could remember seeing in the car at the car wash. An officer was sent over to see if they could retrieve anything from the trash.

"Besides the pen, there were crayons and lollipops," she said. "Renee also said that some cassette tapes we found weren't hers." She stopped to think. "And, oh, there was an old local newspaper, but I don't know from when." She swallowed hard.

"I paid extra for a thorough vacuuming, and made sure they didn't miss anything," she added, barely able to speak above a whisper. "And, here's the worst part. I made sure that they washed the dashboard and the steering wheel, because they were sticky."

Dominique jumped up and radioed the officer who was checking the car wash to look for the previous day's rags. She radioed back that the trash had been picked up the day before at about noon, and that the rags were already washed. Wally felt her heart drop.

"We'll try to see if we can get any fingerprints anyway," Elliot said. He seemed to be trying to encourage Wally not to feel so bad. "At least we know that there won't be a million of Renee's prints to go through."

"I'm so sorry," Wally said. "Please, if you find anything, let me know."

"Yes, ma'am," Officer Scott said. But she didn't look very hopeful.

Wally went over to the library after she left the police station. She hoped to look through the back copies of the local newspaper to see if there was any reference to Lori. Maybe that was why the old newspaper had been in the car. It was all she had to go on.

She got a stack and sat down to work, working backwards, week by week, through the papers. It only came out once a week, and had only local news in it, but it was strange to go through her life backwards, even so small a part of it.

Going back through the first week of November, then through October and September, she found no references to Lori. But the issue published during the last week of August featured a big picture of her, with her friend Jackie.

It looked like a newsprint version of the picture that she had seen in Sandy's living room. It showed the two girls, side by side, one blond and one brunet, both light-eyed, and it had a caption underneath stating that the girls had been selected to be the head cheerleaders for the coming year.

Something about it struck her as odd, so Wally went over to show the picture to her friend Vicki, who was one of the librarians. Perfectly suited to her job, Vicki loved dispensing information. Many people might have regarded some of that information as gossip, but that was okay with

Wally, as long as it wasn't about the Morrises. "Do you remember this?" she asked.

"Oh, yes," Vicki said. "Poor thing. I remember how upset she was that they got the names reversed in the caption. It was a terrible tragedy to her at the time. She begged them to fix it." The local newspaper, often referred to by the local residents as a rag, was known for inaccuracies and political bias. Depending on who the managing editor was, the paper hovered somewhere between borderline acceptable and downright offensive. But many people in town bought it anyway, to read about upcoming events and people they knew. "And now look," Vicki added sadly. "It kind of puts things in their proper perspective, doesn't it?"

Wally nodded in agreement. "I remember seeing this at the time," Wally said, still wondering if this was a copy of the paper she had thrown out, "but I didn't see it in any of the papers afterward."

"I know. They wouldn't print a correction. But she came in a few days later, and she mentioned that they had given her and Jackie a copy of the real photo, and that was almost as good."

"I've seen that. But it doesn't have the captions on it."

"Go figure a teenager. At least she was happy. But now look." Her face resumed its worried expression. "It doesn't sound like the police have any leads."

Wally did not enlighten her about the fact that she had been responsible for ruining some of the leads that they did have. "Maybe they'll get lucky."

"It's been so long, though." Vicki looked down the counter and saw that she was needed. "I have to go. Take care."

Wally went over to the photocopier and inserted a dime. Then she copied the article, picture and all. Maybe this was what had been in the car. Maybe it was something.

As soon as she got home and made sure that things were

going all right in her own little world, Wally called the police station again.

Elliot sounded a lot more hopeful than he had earlier. "We've matched some prints that were on the bottom of the passenger seat to Lori. She was definitely in the car."

"You did? How did you get Lori's fingerprints?"

"From her room. Her parents are excited. They think we're on to something."

Despite her guilt, Wally caught his enthusiasm. "It was the pen. We're lucky they recognized it. But how can you be sure when she was in the car?"

"Both Mr. and Mrs. Nichols swore they didn't even know Lori, so it must have been sometime since the car was stolen, and possibly after she was kidnapped. We're checking the other prints now, to see if we can find out who was with her. We used the prints you gave us to eliminate yours and Mrs. Nichols gave us a set of prints so that we can eliminate hers. She promised her husband would be by later to give us his. We'll need to see if we can get the prints of all the other people who may have been in the car, including the guys at the car wash, so it'd be a real long shot if we could isolate the prints of the person who took Lori. But believe me, this is a big lead."

"That's great. Listen, Elliot, the reason I called was that I found something. I went to the library to try to figure out why that newspaper might have been in the car, because Renee was sure it wasn't in there when the car was stolen. She doesn't buy it unless one of her children's pictures are in it."

"What did you find out?"

"I saw a picture of Lori and Jackie, the same one that was in Lori's house. But when it was printed in the news-paper, the names underneath were reversed. Do you think that Jackie was the target?"

"Why would she be?"

"Why would Lori be? And think about how secretive Jackie's mother was. I wish I could figure this out."

"Me too. I'll think about it. Maybe the reason will come to me. And I'll let you know if we find any more prints."

"Thanks, Elliot. It makes me feel better after I was so stupid."

"You couldn't possibly have known. Wait. Hold on a minute. I have another call."

Wally heard a click. She was tempted to hang up, since she was finished with the conversation, but thought that might be rude. She walked over to the oven, stretching the phone cord, and checked on her dinner.

Elliot was back on the line in a minute, but his voice, so confident before, quivered now. "We just got a call from the police in Allentown. They found the body of a man near the rest stop where Mrs. Nichols's car was found. He was dumped along the side of the road. He's been dead for several days. The police checked the rest stop and his Ford was missing."

"That's terrible," Wally said, when she got her breath back. "When did it happen?"

"They think it happened on Wednesday night, based on what his wife said, and they called us because they knew that a stolen car from this town was recovered in the same area at around that time. Of course, they had no way of knowing that we think the car was involved in Lori's disappearance."

It took a while for Wally to speak. "Did he die the same way as that poor boy?"

"Brian Lambert? Yes. They're sure he was stabbed, probably by a hunting knife. It may be a link, but it's a long shot."

"But it's possible that it was the same person. And he's heading west, and he might have Lori with him. And even if she is okay, she might have seen everything."

"If she is with him, and he's the murderer, we know she's not safe, if that's what you mean. But we know which way they are going and what they are driving. We can widen our search teams, because now the police in Pennsylvania are also involved."

Wally knew that the road intersected with several other highways not far past Allentown. There was no way to know where they were headed.

The picture of the two girls went round and round in Wally's head for the rest of the evening. The nagging feeling that there was some special significance to the newspaper in the car refused to leave her. She put it off for a while, but finally picked up the phone and called Elliot at home. All she got was his answering machine, so she left a message for him to call.

Then she called Louise to see how things had gone with the Kaufmans. For what she considered obvious reasons, she was too embarrassed to call them herself. She did not think they would have been told about how she destroyed possible evidence, but she still couldn't face calling them.

"No problem," Louise said. "I got them everything they needed. It made me feel good, like I was helping in some way. I got a taste of what it must be like to be you, always helping everyone. One thing puzzled me, though. They told me that you had to go to the police station, but they didn't exactly know why."

Wally explained as best she could, minimizing, to her further guilt, her role in undermining the investigation. Nate had told her to stop being so hard on herself, but somehow she could not.

"Sandy and Jeff are hoping that it'll lead to something," Louise said cheerfully. "You and Elliot Levine will be heroes."

It took a few minutes, but Wally was finally able to get her upbeat friend off the phone. She felt like anything but a hero.

When the phone rang a half hour later, Wally was calmer. It was Elliot, returning her call.

"I was at school," he explained. "But to tell you the truth, I was having trouble concentrating. I kept wondering if the 'regular car' that the girl we interviewed described, with such maddening vagueness, was Mrs. Nichols's Volvo."

"I guess it could have been," Wally said. "There are so many of them around here."

"I'll go ask her tomorrow," Elliot said. "Now what can I do for you?"

"I was wondering if there was anything in Lori's diary about the article and picture in the paper. She was very worked up about it, according to one of the librarians, and she may have mentioned it."

"I'll check that tomorrow," Elliot said. "It feels like we might have some real leads for a change."

Chapter Thirteen

Debbie called the first thing the next morning. "I'm thinking of coming out for a visit," she said. "How would you like to make dinner for your daughter?"

"You want to come tonight?" Wally asked. She looked over at Nate and mouthed Debbie's name. "It would be lovely, but it's so unexpected."

"How about if I sleep over too? I can still get to school in time in the morning."

"Of course you can sleep here," Wally said, partially repeating Debbie's words so Nate could keep up with the conversation. "But is something wrong? Is it your room-mate?"

"Nothing like that," Debbie assured her. "I just miss the old neighborhood."

Nate gestured to Wally that he would pick Debbie up at the station. The movements he made involved an imaginary steering wheel, a lot of pointing and a gathering motion, finished up by Nate pointing at his watch with a questioning look on his face.

"Okay. What train will you be on? Your father wants to pick you up."

Debbie laughed. "Always the same old Dad."

"Uh-huh," Wally said, carefully not repeating Debbie's reference to Nate's age.

"I'll be in at six-thirty."

"He'll be there."

Somehow Wally waited to call Elliot until the children in her class went for their music period at 10:00. She promised herself that she would not meddle, but she planned one way or another to find a clever way to work the fact that Debbie would be in town into the conversation. How to do it in a subtle manner was the big question.

"I went over the diary," Elliot said.

"What did it say?" Wally asked.

"Lori wrote about the mix-up. At first she was annoyed, but then she thought it was funny, at least until a stranger came up to her, and called her 'Jackie.' Even then she didn't think too much about it, she wrote, but a few days later he came again, and said something about it being too long since he'd seen her, and so she told him that she was Lori. But then he said he'd know her anywhere, and he tried to touch her hair. She said she got scared and walked away. That was the entry we'd originally read about the stranger."

"I can understand her being frightened by that," Wally said. "I wonder why she didn't tell Sandy about it."

"She wrote that she felt silly afterwards, and that Jackie told her it was nothing. He was probably only trying to touch a star."

"That's ridiculous," Wally said. "I guess she thinks that being head cheerleader makes a person famous."

"Maybe." Elliot's voice was tight. "We've started trying to track down this stranger. We're going to try to talk to Jackie about it today."

"It sounds like she could be part of all of this. I would like to know what she said," Wally said. "I wish I knew her, so that I could ask her some questions myself."

"I'm sure you'd like to, Mrs. Morris. But you must leave it to us. We still don't know if there's any connection."

"I know. It's just that I'm so worried about Lori. It could have been anyone . . ." Wally took a deep breath. "Maybe even one of my daughters." As the tension of wondering how to mention Debbie left her, she mentally gave herself a pat on the back.

"How are they?" Elliot asked, as he walked into her web.

"Rachel is terrific." Wally paused. "Oh, and Debbie will be coming out to visit us tonight, by dinner time."

"That's nice," Elliot said. "How about if I give you a call if anything else comes up?"

"That would be fine." Wally smiled as she said goodbye. She had a strong feeling she might hear from Elliot that evening.

She had just hung up the phone when it rang. No one was in the nursery school office, so she answered it.

The person on the line asked Wally to bring Timmy to the phone. The voice was a man's, and sounded tense. Wally had the sense that it was the child's father, and that if his mother knew, she would rush over to take the boy out of the school, most likely for good. She did not want his father to find him, or take him away.

Speaking as firmly as she could, Wally told the man that children could not be called to the telephone.

"What time do the children get out of school?" he asked.

"At two-thirty," Wally said, although that wasn't the time that Timmy left. Only those children in the extended day program stayed until 2:30. She had stretched the truth, but hopefully had also given Timmy's mother time to pick him up and get him away, if that was what she wanted. It was a tough situation.

As soon as the man hung up, Wally made another call—to Timmy's mother.

Elliot and Dominique spent the morning questioning Tiffany, the girl who could not distinguish cars, about the Volvo. When he showed her the picture she made a positive ID, but she still couldn't give any further description of the driver.

They were unable to schedule an appointment to speak to Jackie Gibson. Although she was back in school, Mrs. Gibson had requested that no one be allowed to question her daughter without her being present. The school had no choice but to respect her wishes.

It was frustrating. The police in Pennsylvania had not been able to trace the dead man's stolen car, and it was generally assumed that it had left the state. It could have gone to New York, or Maryland, or West Virginia, or Ohio, or even Delaware. And the likelihood that the driver would once again want to change cars, as well as the method he might use to do it, worried Elliot. He was sure that Mrs. Nichols was unaware of the fact that she was mighty lucky that she was not killed when her car was stolen.

That was strange, all in all. The fact that the car was in town at least a few times, over a period of almost two months, did not say much for the detective work of the police force. It was little consolation that it had different license plates and was, as Tiffany put it, a 'regular car.' Apparently, now that he had his quarry, he was changing cars, trying to elude police.

Elliot said goodbye to Dominique at 6:35 and decided to swing by Mrs. Morris's to let her know about the girl's identification of the car before he went to his evening classes. He arrived just as Debbie was getting out of her father's car.

Wally watched from the kitchen window as Elliot greeted Nate and Debbie. He looked awkward, but he had a big smile on his face. Cracking the window, Wally strained to hear their conversation.

Debbie smiled back at Elliot and said a shy hello, but Nate smiled warmly and put out his gloved hand to shake Elliot's. "How are you doing, young man?"

"Very good, sir."

"Did you find out something else? My wife has been very concerned."

"Nothing much, sir, but I thought she'd like to know."

"It's cold out here," Mr. Morris said. "Come inside. I'm sure she'd like to hear any news."

As Elliot helped Debbie carry her overnight case into the house, Wally went to set another place at the table for their guest.

There it was, an excellent car for him to change into. It was dark enough outside, and quiet, a weekday evening with all the little ants back in their little ant holes, finished with their little ant jobs, leaving little in the way of traffic.

He drove along slowly. She was asleep in the seat next to him, and with any luck she would stay that way. It would be better if she did not see this, not again.

She had not spoken a single word since he picked her up. It was a week already, but he was being a patient man. They said he had an anger management problem, those prison shrinks, and before them the army shrink who had so unfairly given him a dishonorable discharge had said the same thing, but he would show them he could hold it together. For her at least. He knew she would come around, and admit that she was happy to be with him. Meanwhile, he talked to her.

She had struggled against him, he remembered. That had really hurt his feelings. He did not like thinking that she felt that way. But she had not tried to run away, not since that college boy got in the way, the one who made him use his knife. Where did he come off interfering anyway? He had no use for people who got in his way.

Uh-oh, he thought. There was the owner of the car. Too bad. He had hoped to have the car hot-wired before she returned. But this would be better, because then he would have the keys for the trunk. He could just transfer the girl, and all the food he had brought, which was a considerable amount. They couldn't exactly stop off along the way, not so soon, anyway. After the exchange they would be off again.

He parked in the space next to the car he wanted. It was a Toyota Camry, pretty common around these parts, but he knew he would have to get an American car before he got further into the Midwest. They might stick out too much otherwise, but for now this would be good. He had always wanted to drive one.

The woman turned the key in the door lock, and he noticed that a light on the top center of the dashboard went out. Evidently, the car had an alarm. Well then, it was a mighty good thing he would have the keys.

He had already stolen another set of license plates, and as soon as he could he would pull off the road and change them with the ones on the car. The Camry was local, from Ohio, but he would switch the plates with a set from New York. No problem. After turning off the dome light so that she wouldn't notice him, he opened his door quietly, and crouched down.

As soon as the woman turned around to back her little rear end into the car, he was on her. He slipped his knife into the area of her heart and held her mouth until she sank to the ground. She was so light, and, in the glow from the overhead lamp, young. The woman was kind of pretty too, but that was a pity, since she was almost dead.

He dragged her behind some bushes, and quickly transferred the food from the Ford. Then he woke the girl, and told her they were changing cars again. She seemed very frightened as she went, still silent, into the Camry, but he would bring her around. Soon.

* * *

Ohio state trooper Ronald McCarthy arrived at the scene at the rest stop on route 80/90 while the young woman's body was still warm. His preliminary investigation revealed that a curious poodle found it in a clump of bushes while his family was taking a break from their journey to Grandma's in Chicago. That family stood huddled together now, wishing more than anything that they had left the dog in a boarding kennel.

Officer McCarthy briefly wondered if it was the missing girl from New Jersey, but this woman had auburn hair, at this moment partially across her face, concealing her death mask. A thin trench coat covered her business suit.

There was a big accident several miles east that tied up all the available ambulances and other personnel. McCarthy allowed the poodle and its family to leave, but the body had to stay where it was, growing colder every minute.

By the time it was picked up and brought to the morgue, most of the police staff had left for the day. The tired young officer hoped they would get lucky and get a missing persons report on the young woman before he knocked himself out trying to determine who she was.

He figured the body would keep until the next day. But he made sure to list it and the car, as a last minute what-the-heck before he punched out for the day, on the crime reports that went out nationwide.

"Would you like some more?" Wally asked, holding up a serving spoonful of stew. "There's plenty."

It had been lucky that Elliot's classes were cancelled for the evening and he could accept the dinner invitation. Now, she waited as Elliot weighed the pros and cons of another helping. When he agreed to have some more, she served him a half plateful. It would not do to over-stuff him, because then he would want to go home to relax.

Debbie was barely eating, Wally noticed, and this had always been one of her favorite dishes. The way she gazed at Elliot, however, confirmed to Wally that her daughter was distracted, not just because of a slight alteration in the recipe, but because she had more to think about.

Watching Debbie and Elliot, Wally thought they looked very cute together, and she was even more convinced that something other than her stew was cooking, especially when Debbie leaned forward provocatively to talk to Elliot as he wiped the gravy from his plate with a piece of rye bread. Wally glanced over at Nate to see if he noticed. He kept his eyes averted from her, on purpose, she was sure. Never mind him. She knew.

Too bad there was no way Wally could ever bring up the subject with her daughter, unless Debbie brought it up first, and even then, she'd never get a straight answer about her feelings. All Wally could do was wait and hope.

"You sit," she said to Debbie, after they had all finished. "Your Dad can help me." She rose, and brought several plates into the kitchen. Nate dutifully followed her lead.

About a minute later they heard Debbie call out. "We're going out to walk off dinner," she said. "We'll take Sammy."

"Okay," Wally called back. She waited until she heard the jingle of the leash followed by the slam of a door and then went over every nuance between Elliot and Debbie with Nate. He smiled an amused smile, in that annoyingly indulgent way he had, as she went on and on. "And I'm betting we'll have an extra person at our Thanksgiving table."

"We'll see," Nate said.

It was a relief to stop thinking about Lori for a few hours. They had not even discussed it, which was kind of odd, especially when Nate reminded her, just after Wally finished planning the wedding, that Elliot originally stopped by to talk about the case. No wonder Nate's eyes were twinkling.

*   *   *

It was very late when Elliot got back into his house. He checked the machine and saw that there was a message. "This is Palmeri." He was the night dispatch sergeant. "I thought you should know that a car matching the description of the one that was reported stolen out of Allentown has turned up in Ohio, with another body next to it. It's a woman, but not your girl, from the description. We won't have any more details until morning, but I've sent a request for hair and fingerprint analysis of the car to see if we get a match with the Kaufman girl. And the press seems to have lost patience with us. All the networks and newspapers have said that they will go public starting tomorrow morning. Sorry. Have a good one." Beep.

Chapter Fourteen

At 6:30 A.M. Wally had a rude awakening: Nate's clock radio blaring loudly. Nate was already up and in the shower so that he could drive Debbie to the 7:30 train. Without getting out of bed, or at least swimming over to Nate's side, Wally could not reach the radio and turn it down. She lay still, trying to ignore the noise and enjoy the few minutes she had before she had to get up.

Toward the end of the news segment, the broadcaster mentioned Lori Kaufman. It seemed impossible, given the promised news blackout, and for a second Wally thought she might be mistaken, that the story was about someone else. As she listened, however, she had confirmation of the worst kind. The story had broken. She threw Nate's pillow over his radio to mute it and switched on the TV just in time to catch a segment of the local news.

"Good morning," the newscaster said with a smile. "Here's what's happening in the New York metropolitan area today." He replaced his smile with a serious, almost disapproving expression. "A little over a week ago, in quiet Grosvenor," he pronounced it Grove Ner, the English way, which made Wally bristle at his ignorance, "New Jersey, a young man was found stabbed to death. Although there are few leads in that case, there is evidence to suggest that another crime, one not reported in the media," here he paused to indicate his outrage that the media had been excluded from something that was clearly in their province to report, "was related."

File footage was shown. It was the same one that had played over and over the previous week. But it was followed by an exterior view of first the high school and then the Kaufman home.

"Oh, no!" Wally said, and then clamped her hand over her mouth. She hoped she had not awakened Debbie, but the horror of seeing Lori's story on the air was almost too much. Nate came out of the bathroom, his face full of shaving cream on the left side, clean shaven on the right, with just a little of the foam in his right ear. He sat down on the edge of the bed, next to Wally, and together they watched as the story was revealed.

A reporter's voice-over told about the disappearance of Lori Kaufman the previous week, and showed a picture of her, along with height and weight statistics and a description of what she was last seen wearing. Then there was a short piece about Brian Lambert, who was referred to as a student at the local college, and the fact that on the night that Lori disappeared, he was murdered. No direct correlation was made except for the very fact that the stories were being presented together. Finally, the car thefts and murder of one of the owners were mentioned as being connected.

Suddenly the face of the morning news person replaced the image on the screen, now with a very somber look on his face. "Our sources tell us that police this hour are saying that a second and third car theft and possibly two other murders are being linked to this crime spree. They are desperately seeking leads to catch this person before another crime is committed." Wally turned off the TV.

Lori's disappearance and that boy's murder and now these other killings were almost too much to bear. She felt totally drained. "Bodies keep turning up."

Nate put his arm around her shoulder. "None is Lori. I think she's still okay."

Wally looked at him critically. "I wish I thought you believed that. Even if it is true, why is this happening? And how long will she be 'okay'?"

At school, Wally found that she was distracted. One of the children had to ask her three times to go to the bathroom before she realized that he was talking to her. "I'm sorry, sweetie," she apologized. "Let's hurry." She helped him get his jeans down and sit on the tiny porcelain toilet, while admonishing herself to pay attention.

By the time school let out, though, she freely gave her thoughts over to her feelings. Something nagged at her, more significant than a missed birthday card, even more than a thoughtless comment. She focused on that while she was driving home.

Suddenly it came to her. She turned her car around, and headed over to Renee Nichols's house.

She stopped in front, right behind the blue Volvo station wagon. Before ringing the bell, Wally took a minute to inspect the car.

When she'd had it cleaned, she noticed that the door locks had no scratches near them. That was what had disturbed her. The car might not have been broken into when it was stolen. It could have been unlocked, she supposed, but how would it have been started? Nate hadn't said anything about it being hot-wired.

Renee answered the door in a frenzy and Wally could hear babies crying in the background.

"I'm terribly sorry to come without calling," Wally said, "but I have to ask you a question about your car."

"Really? Okay, sure." Her lack of annoyance at being asked more questions made Wally wonder if the interruption, by an adult, had been at least a bit welcome.

"I know this may make you nervous, but I really need an honest answer. Whatever it is, I won't tell Nate."

Renee's face was blank.

Wally launched into her question. "Did you leave the keys in the car before it was stolen? Or maybe you had an extra key hidden on the car?"

Renee dipped her head. "I've heard the news. I know I could've been killed, like those others." She looked up and Wally could see tears in her eyes. "I swear, I didn't leave the key in the car, and I've never had one of those hidden keys. I still have my original key right here on my key ring. Look, I'll show you."

She pulled the keys out of her pocket and handed them over, at the same time confiding, "I never take the keys out of my pocket during the day. One of my kids once accidentally locked me out of the house when I took out the garbage and I had to get the fire department to get me back in. It was awful." She wiped at a tear but somehow managed a smile.

Wally burst out laughing. "I'm sorry. I wasn't laughing at you. That once happened to me."

She took a second to make sure that Renee had calmed down before examining the keys. There were two types of car keys on the two-sided detachable ring, a set for a Saab as well as the Volvo set, and several house keys. Both sets looked like originals to Wally, who had seen copies made over the years for each of her children.

Although Wally wracked her brain, she couldn't remember what key was in it the day she took it to the car wash. "What key was in the car when you got it back?"

"A new one, I guess. I didn't think about it. The ignition key didn't have the usual Volvo insignia on it, though. It's plain and ugly. I have it in the kitchen if you want to see it. Do you want to come in?"

The sound of crying helped Wally make a decision. "I'll just stay here."

"I don't blame you."

Wally was wondering what this new piece of information could mean when Renee came back with a shiny new key.

"Does this help?" she asked.

"I don't know. I wish I knew where it came from." Another thought occurred to her. "What if . . . Could you tell me if you left your car, with your key, anywhere just before it was stolen?"

"Gee, that was a long time ago. Like where?"

"Did you maybe leave it with a valet?"

Renee giggled. "Why of course, darling," she said mimicking a high society stereotype. "I went to Bloomingdale's and had them park it for me while I spent the day frolicking in the mall." Her sarcasm went deep.

Chastised, Wally asked, "Did you have any work done on the car?"

"You know," she said, "I did take it to have the oil changed. I went over to one of those places that does it super fast, which is about all the time I have."

"Which place?"

"The one on Springfield."

Wally thanked her and left, determined to follow her lead even though her stomach was crying out for sustenance.

Elliot was unable to conceal his feelings from Dominique. "I know this case is getting more complicated," she said. "But you can't let it get to you."

"I can't get over the fact that if we had done something sooner, those other people wouldn't be dead."

"We did everything we could," Dominique said soothingly. "We'll catch him."

Elliot knew that the idea of beating out all those other

investigators from different states and branches of law enforcement appealed to his partner. As it was, they were having difficulty keeping up with all the requests for information from everyone. On top of that, Captain Jaeger kept insisting that no matter how many people were investigating, his department had to be involved. He drew in a deep breath and let it puff out his cheeks as he expelled it. "But now it's in the press."

Yet another phone rang. Dominique sighed, as much agreeing with Elliot as offering sympathy for their situation. They could no longer shield the girl's parents and the town from the media. Additional staff was required to handle the crackpot calls they had started to get as soon as the story hit the news. Calls had gone out for more police officers to keep up with the added traffic on the streets, and the high school had sent a request for another security officer to keep the press out of the school.

"He could decide to change cars again," Elliot said. "And someone else could die."

"At least it looks like Lori is still alive," Dominique said.

Elliot fought to control his emotions. "Why? Because no one has found her body? That doesn't exactly inspire confidence in me. Now her parents will realize that there may have been other murders related to this. They can't help but be more frightened."

"Maybe we'll get some confirmation of Lori being alive when they give us the lab results of the abandoned car, if it really is connected as we think. We'll get him. He's leaving a trail." Dominique sounded positive, or like she was trying to sound positive. "And we've got a lot of high-powered support."

"What worries me the most is . . ." Elliot paused, searching for a phrase, "don't you think that eventually he is going to get wherever it is he is going, and hole up? Then how would we find him? He could do what he did to those people on the highway." He shook his head. "Which sounds a lot like what happened to Brian Lambert."

"I feel terrible for that family," Dominique said. "It must seem as if we aren't even trying to find the killer."

"We aren't on that investigation anymore," Elliot said, in defense of both of them. "And I did promise his aunt I would call if we had anything."

"I'm not feeling guilty, if that's what you think I meant," Dominique said. "But I'm getting frustrated."

Elliot wished there was some way to help the county. "If we can prove a connection, we'd be assisting in the murder investigation," he reasoned.

"But how?"

Elliot was saved from having to answer that by his phone.

Mrs. Morris was on the line, speaking very fast. "Could you repeat that, Mrs. Morris?" he asked, turning away from Dominique's frown.

"I'll be right there," he said. Before he had hung up the phone, he'd grabbed his jacket. "I just got a lead," he told Dominique. "Maybe this is it."

Elliot went over the conversation with Mrs. Morris as he raced down the corridor leading to the parking lot. Dominique followed right behind.

"Mrs. Morris asked me if I really said that Renee Nichols was lucky not to have been killed for her car."

Dominique caught up to Elliot. "And?"

"She's a sharp little lady."

"Why do you say that?"

"She realized that we never really investigated the theft, beyond the usual checklist."

"Was she accusing the department of poor police work?"

"No," Elliot said, holding the door for his partner. "She said she wasn't looking to pin blame on anyone. She just needed to know."

"What did you tell her?"

"That it was just assumed that it was stolen from in front of her house. That's what the records say."

Elliot got into the police cruiser's driver's seat and leaned out the window. "Mrs. Morris told me that according to Renee, when they recovered the car, they found a key in it."

Dominique's eyebrows lifted. "She left her keys in the car?"

"No, that's just it. Mrs. Morris found out she still had the keys with her. She had them the whole time the car was gone. I'm going to check it out now."

"Good luck," Dominique said. "I'll take care of things here."

Elliot peeled out of the parking lot, thinking about what Mrs. Morris had said next, the reason for his excitement.

"I think," she'd said, "I might know how that happened, but I need your help."

She had explained where she was, and Elliot hurried to get there.

Chapter Fifteen

Elliot wished he could put the siren on and zoom over to the Spot Oil station. It took a lot of effort to show some restraint, and he tried to divert his impatience. He thought about Dominique, and one of the things she had said earlier.

"You're embarrassed about suspecting those boys."

It had surprised Elliot that his partner was able to put a name on the uncomfortable feeling that he'd had. In self-defense he'd said, "There was evidence that Zach might have done it. And you said yourself that Lori was really interested in Hull."

Dominique shook her head. "A teenage diary is not a pleasant place to visit, and I can say that even though I was once a teenager."

"Not so long ago," Elliot reminded her. "But you're right. I guess I am kind of embarrassed. Especially since it was Mrs. Morris who got it straightened out."

"Notwithstanding the fact that she has actually helped us, I still don't understand why you tell her so much. I thought you weren't interested in her daughter."

Elliot smiled. "Not her elder daughter. But her other daughter is a knockout."

"Ah," Dominique responded, smiling.

Elliot had looked away after seeing the expression on his partner's face. No one had a right to look that satisfied.

Now it seemed to Elliot as if Mrs. Morris was also actively helping their investigation. He wondered if she really had a lead.

He got to Spot Oil in less than five minutes and ran into the office.

"They said they have a key-making machine," Wally reported, an angry look on her face. "But they won't tell me anything else. Maybe the manager will talk to you."

The manager, whose name was George, according to the embroidery on his shirt, was a big swarthy man with bulging muscles. "Do you mean this lady is serious?"

Elliot nodded. "We need to check on employees who might have quit or been fired any time from right after Mrs. Nichols's car was serviced up until last week."

As George went to find the information, Wally looked vindicated. "I was thinking about this all morning before I called you," she explained. "It didn't add up."

George returned almost immediately. He handed them two computer printouts, one listing customers, and one listing employees. While they looked at it, he stabbed an oil-stained finger at one of the pages and shook his head. "It don't look like very good news, I'm afraid. We had this one guy who started working here on a Monday morning, the day that Mrs. Nichols came in, and he was gone after lunch. He just never came back. I remember that. It ain't unheard of, lotsa guys do it. They don't like working here or something." George seemed amazed that anyone would give up a job there.

"What was his name?" Mrs. Morris asked. "And what did he look like?"

"Is it okay to talk in front of her? She ain't a cop, is she?" His expression was one of disbelief as he assessed the tiny woman in front of him.

"No, but I guess she's earned the right to hear it," Elliot said.

George thought about it for a minute, while he idly scratched his left elbow with a grimy fingernail. "Oh, let's see. His name is Richards, Karl Richards." He waited, patiently watching while Elliot wrote that down in his notebook, before continuing. "He was a white guy, about five-ten I'd say, with blond, stringy hair pulled back in a ponytail. But he didn't have no earring. I hate those things. I don't hire no guys with earrings.

"Most guys, though," George continued, "even when they're quitting, they expect to be paid for the time they were here, every second. But not him."

Elliot thought that was odd. "He didn't even come in for his pay for the half day?"

"No. And we got to pay it. That's our company policy, so we mailed it to him. But it came back, marked 'addressee unknown'."

"Do you have the address anyway?" Mrs. Morris asked. "Maybe we could check it out."

Feeling like he should be more in charge of this investigation than the nursery school teacher beside him, Elliot added, "And can I get a copy of his application? Anything you have would be helpful."

George ran off a copy of several papers and handed them over. The address was in one of the towns in the next county. "Thanks," Elliot said. He turned to Mrs. Morris and said, as firmly as he could, "I'll take it from here."

He was feeling more hopeful than he had in days.

Driving home, hoping to hear if Elliot had found anything from her lead, Wally could not remember when she felt so nervous. It was compounded, now that the news was out, by the feeling that her town was under siege. Media trucks were everywhere and reporters looking for information from residents stood on street corners with their microphones ever-ready for interviews.

At home, Wally told Nate about her part in the investigation. She had expected him to be proud of her, but his reaction was quite the opposite.

"You shouldn't be pestering that poor detective," Nate said. "He has work to do."

"Were you listening when I told you that I found a lead?"

Nate's expression was skeptical. "We'll see."

Seething, Wally could barely look at him, but her hostility faded while he told her what had been on the noon news. In addition to the coverage they had shown in the morning, they had interviews with several high-schoolers testifying to their undying affection for Lori, their certainty that she wouldn't run away, and their fears for themselves. Then there was a brief interview with the police director. B.J. Waters was back after that, attempting to interview Sandy and Jeff, but they refused to speak before the cameras.

When Nate went back to his office, Wally tried to call Elliot. Someone else answered his phone, said that Elliot wasn't there, and asked if she wanted to leave a message. Wally declined. She hung up, took half of the leftover stew from the previous night's dinner, and instead of freezing it, packed it to go with an extra loaf of rye bread she'd stored in the freezer. She felt as if she had redeemed herself with the Kaufmans somewhat, and that she had earned another visit with Sandy.

She parked around the corner, as usual. But this time she cut across the yard to the back door, since the front door and most of the sidewalk out front were full of reporters.

Sandy peeked out the window through the curtain, and when she saw Wally, she held up her hand. Wally heard the sound of a dead bolt turning as Sandy let her in.

"I'm sorry. I don't usually leave that lock closed when we're in the house," she explained. "But it's been horrible.

And now all these reporters want to talk about it and speculate about where Lori could be and . . ."

"I know. I'm so sorry. But don't give up hope."

"It isn't easy," Sandy said. "I wish I knew what to do."

Wally could not respond to that, which made her feel inadequate yet again. She handed the stew and bread to Sandy, who gratefully accepted.

"You're too good to us. We can never repay you."

"You don't need to. I wish I could do more."

"Everyone does. It was so nice of Louise to shop for us after you had to leave. Meanwhile, I feel utterly useless just sitting here. I keep going over and over things in my mind, trying to remember if Lori said anything about a stranger, but I can't recall. I asked Felice if her sister said anything. She practically squeezed every thought out of her head, but she couldn't remember anything. And I tried to ask Jackie, the last time she called, but she didn't answer me, and she hasn't called back since then."

That surprised Wally. "I thought she called frequently."

"She did, but after I asked her about a stranger, she stopped."

"It sounds to me like she really knows something, and I keep getting the feeling that it's tied into the mixed-up pictures." Wally took a minute to remind Sandy about how the girls' names were reversed under their pictures.

"I remember that," Sandy said. "Lori was really upset. But the paper wouldn't straighten it out. They gave her and Jackie each a good quality picture. You saw it, didn't you?"

Wally nodded.

"And I thought Lori would be happy with that. In fact, she said she was, but I had the feeling that something was still bothering her about it."

She picked up the tea kettle and went to the sink to fill it. "Would you like a cup of tea? Or maybe coffee?"

"No thanks," Wally said. "I have to be going. I'll check back with you soon."

* * *

Elliot's hopes faded when he discovered that there was no such address on the street that Karl Richards had listed as his home. He had called Dominique with the particulars that Richards had listed on his job application, but a quick check of the computers at the police station turned up nothing. Absolutely all the information was phony. They drove around the area anyway, looking for anything that could help them.

"It looks like he was only there to get access to a car," Elliot said. "He was probably just waiting for the right one, to get a copy of the key, and the address where it could be found."

"It sounds that way," Dominique said. "Mrs. Morris was pretty sharp to pick up this lead."

Her voice sounded funny. "Are you jealous?" Elliot asked.

"In a way. It seems so obvious now." She went through the papers that the Spot Oil manager had given to Elliot. "The date of the work order for Mrs. Nichols car was right around the time that picture of Lori was in the paper. That's another reason to link him to Lori's disappearance. If only we'd known." She was silent for a second. "Well, at least we have this now. I wonder . . ."

"What?"

"Well, your friend Mrs. Morris seems convinced that it points to Jackie somehow."

Elliot, whose eyes were fixed on the road, nodded without looking at his partner. "She may be right. But we can't get through to Jackie with that mother of hers guarding her. I'm going to put in for a court order."

"If that's what it takes," Dominique said. "We have a description of Karl Richards. Let's run it through the computer and see what we come up with. It's worth a try."

Elliot turned the car in the direction of the police station. "Okay."

* * *

It was 3:00 when Wally drove over to Louise's house. When she turned onto the street, Michelle, Louise's daughter, was just closing the door behind herself. Wally parked in front of the Tudor house and got out.

She rang the bell and waited until the door was opened. "My mom isn't home," Michelle said, when she saw who was on the doorstep. She munched on an apple, smacking her lips as she took a bite.

"Can I come in for a minute?" Wally asked. "I wanted to talk to you."

"Okay, I guess," Michelle said, pulling her flannel shirt closed over her t-shirt to ward off the chill from the doorway. She seemed lethargic as she invited Wally inside and led her into the living room. "What do you want to talk about?"

Wally took a deep breath. "I know you're not really good friends with Jackie Gibson, but I think she might know something about Lori's disappearance, and I was hoping you could help."

Suddenly energized, Michelle leaned forward from her perch on the arm of her mother's couch. "You mean you think she knows where Lori is and won't say? That's horrible. Lori is her best friend!"

"I don't think she knows where Lori is, exactly, but she might know something. Do you remember the picture of Lori and Jackie that was in the newspaper?"

The apple hung poised in the air as the teenager looked blankly at Wally.

"The one where their names were reversed."

"Oh, yeah. What about it?"

"I've been wondering about it. Apparently someone thought that Lori was Jackie. But that doesn't make any sense. Anyone who knows them knows that Jackie has dark hair and Lori is blond."

Michelle nodded her own mane of orange hair. "That's true. But . . . Oh! Maybe I didn't tell you!"

"Tell me what?"

"I did! I told you about Jackie and the horse and the barn, didn't I?" The apple was finished, and the core slowly turned brown as Michelle held it pinched between her left forefinger and thumb. "I'm sure I told you. That was when you said you had a barn and I said I knew, but that Jackie really was from the Midwest."

"I remember. You said that Jackie was wearing braids and sitting on a pony in front of a barn."

"Didn't I tell you that her hair was blond?"

Wally was stunned. "No. Are you sure it was Jackie? Her hair is so dark."

"Yes. I'm positive. She had blond hair. I guess it got darker."

Wally thought back to her former nursery school student, Emily. Her hair had become much darker than it was when she was younger.

"But it still doesn't make sense." Wally was thinking out loud. "Why would someone think she still had light hair, unless he hadn't seen her in a long time?"

"He?" said Michelle. "They're sure it's a man?"

"I guess so. He seems to be killing other people to take their cars. Not many women would do that."

Michelle shuddered.

"I have to go now," Wally said. "Could you please give your mother my regards?"

"Sure," the teenager said. Then she looked at Wally. "This is really creepy."

"I know."

She still would not say a word, and it was beginning to get to him. She just sat stiffly in her seat, when she was not sleeping, which she did more than any other person he had ever seen. When she was awake, though, she alternated between glaring at him, and seeming terrified. It was hard to say which was worse.

Karl was sorry that he had to insist that she not use the rest stops along the road. All he could do was pull off the road when she needed to relieve herself and hand her a roll of toilet paper. It was obvious that she hated to go in the woods. What girl would like it? Yet he would not take a chance that she might talk to someone in the ladies' room, or even try to run away. He couldn't exactly go into a rest room with her.

It was worse when he had to sleep because then he had to tie her up. He used ropes made out of bed sheets. While he was careful never to make them too tight, he could not take the chance that she would run away.

They always parked in some deserted area while he slept, so he didn't have to worry about her screaming for help. They spent most of their days in deserted areas and abandoned cabins, and some days they didn't drive at all. It was pretty boring, but he had no choice. He could not take the chance of getting there too soon.

It was too bad he had to snatch her so early. Just after he got his hair cut, no, styled, to look respectable, he first saw her, but then it was so long until he saw her again that when the opportunity presented itself he snatched her. It had been a clear shot, almost, and it was the very first time he had seen her alone since that other time, when she had pretended not to know him. That incident had made him pretty mad, almost mad enough to hit something, although of course he would never hit her. And as much as he followed her, hoping that she would turn right around and throw her arms around him and say that she had missed him, she did not. Most of that time he wasn't able to get a clear view of her, so he had gotten her when he could, and traveled real slow, taking his time, since then.

Twice they had checked into a motel. He had to keep her tied up and out of sight while he filled out the forms, and he thought that the desk clerk of the second hotel seemed very suspicious when he paid cash. The desk clerk had looked closely at the name Karl had written on the forms. That day it had been Peter Haygood, an old school buddy. Good ol' Pete. But even if he thought something was fishy, the desk clerk probably assumed he was just shacking up with someone else's wife. He never let anyone see the girl anyway, and besides, if he really thought about it, she was not too young to be married.

It was dangerous to go to any motel, though, so they could not do it often. But he knew she appreciated being able to take a shower in the motel room (after he had made sure she couldn't climb out a window, of course) and sleep in a normal bed, even if she had to be tied up and gagged. He could tell by her eyes that it was worth it, even if she never said anything.

No matter. He kept talking to her about old times. Sooner or later she would come around. And they would be at their destination soon.

It was time to change cars. Hopefully, this would be the last time. He knew this was the worst part for her. Maybe he should try to wait until she was sleeping again. He would have to wait until after dark, anyway. But not too long. He looked at his map, searching for the rest stops along the highway, and made his plans.

Chapter Sixteen

Wally called Elliot as soon as she got home. Their exchange of pleasantries was brief, because Wally wanted to get right to the point. "Did you find him?"

"Not yet." His subsequent summary of the search didn't sound too promising.

"Keep looking," Wally advised. "Now I have something else to think about. When you questioned Jackie at her home, did you see the pictures of her as a child?"

"No. What pictures?"

"Michelle Fisch said there were pictures of Jackie on a pony as a child. I think she said they were in the living room. Didn't you see them?" She chewed her lip nervously, waiting for his answer. He just had to have seen them. It would help to prove her theory.

"As a matter of fact," Elliot said thoughtfully, "I think I saw where they used to be. I remember thinking at the time that there seemed to be pictures missing, because I saw lines in the dust."

Wally did not comment on Mrs. Gibson's housekeeping, but she was frustrated. Then she realized that the pictures

116

just might possibly have been removed in a hurry, which in itself lent support to her idea. "Maybe they took them away."

"Why do you say that?" Elliot asked. "And why are they so important?"

"Michelle mentioned that Jackie used to be blond, like Lori is, and maybe that showed in the pictures. I'm not sure that's important, but I thought it might be."

"I don't see how," Elliot said, "unless you think that 'the stranger' thought that Lori was Jackie because he hadn't seen Jackie since she was a little girl."

"You're following me," Wally said, with satisfaction. "Good. Now how about if I told you that Michelle also said that Jackie's mother had remarried? That would mean that Mr. Gibson is probably not Jackie's biological father."

"You think her real father might be 'the stranger'?" Elliot asked. "But even in divorces, the biological father gets to visit the child. Then he'd know that Jackie's hair was dark, and also what her face looks like now. I'm not really sure that we have anything here."

Despite Elliot's negative attitude, Wally proceeded. "But wait. There's more. Michelle said that Jackie used to live in Nebraska. Maybe he hasn't seen her. Maybe he didn't even know where she was. Maybe Mrs. Gibson was hiding her." She had been thinking of Timmy, the little boy who had been in her class. His mother had pulled him out of the school, and was moving out of state. Wally wondered how the boy's father would feel in the future, if he hadn't seen him in several years, and if he would recognize him. "You've heard of parental kidnapping, right?"

Elliot spoke quickly. "Let me call you right back."

Wally's jaw was clenched as she hung up the phone, and she had to force herself to breathe. She had done what she could. It seemed she was on to something. If only it would help.

*   *   *

Her phone rang five minutes later. It was Elliot. "Mrs. Gibson won't tell me anything about her ex-husband. She said she hasn't seen or heard from him in eight years. She wouldn't even give me his name."

"You have to find out!"

"I know. My partner and I are checking into it."

Wally fought to keep calm. But she couldn't help blurting out, "If I'm right, and this man has the wrong girl, what will he do to her when he finds out? Even if she didn't tell him, it's been all over the news all day!"

At dusk, Karl drove out of the woods onto a dirt lane and followed it along until it came onto a paved road. She was beside him, quiet and wide-eyed, as they drove along the rutted asphalt.

"Just a little ways to the highway, sweetheart," he said. His little girl, right there on the seat next to him after all these years, did not speak a word, but he knew that she loved him. He could see it in her eyes. She was just tired of driving and hiding. That was all.

The child sure had grown since he saw her last. She was a little bit of nothing then, missing her front teeth, but always smiling anyway, except those times when her mother made him mad and he had to punish her. That woman deserved everything she got and more. It was a wonder he managed to stay with that witch for so long. He would have left years before if not for the girl. It sometimes made him almost sorry when he had to show her mother who was boss, because her little face looked so sad. But it had not been like that all the time, like when she had looked so cute those last few days before it happened.

He remembered it all so well, that sweltering, humid day, the kind where the slightest breeze raised the hair on a man's arms and the back of his neck. There was a heavy, overcast sky, and clouds that seemed to want to cry torrents of fat sassy raindrops. It was August third, the blackest day of his life, the day when that brat made him lose everything.

But right before that, during that whole hot week of pure blue cloudless skies and unrelenting sunshine, she had been so smart, so precious, so full of love. He pictured her now, on the day before, August the second, in those little shorts, with a cutoff shirt that did not cover the birthmark she hated so much. He had always told her he loved it, that it reminded him of melted chocolate running from her heart into her belly button, and that she should never be embarrassed, but she did not like it, not one bit.

She had sat on his lap, long into the evening, too pooped to move. Her blond hair had curled up on the edges, trying to pull itself away from her flushed and sweaty freckled face. Eventually she fell asleep, and he carried her in his arms, sweetly dreaming, to her little bed in the house. His nightmare was just about to start, but she stayed unaware of everything until a long time later.

Now she was grown. Well, almost grown, anyway. It amazed him how different she looked. A young lady. A senior in high school. That was two more years of education than he ever had.

Her mother, that witch, had never liked the fact that he didn't graduate from high school and would not let him forget it, not for one single minute, no sir. She harped and nagged and wheedled and totally held out on him. That was the worst. She had insisted that he get an equivalency certificate before she would sleep with him. At the time, it had seemed worth it.

He thought back to how she had looked then, still in high school even though she could have dropped out and had fun like him, at least like he did after he came back from the army. That had been a lot sooner than he thought it would be when he signed up, and there had been no honorable discharge to put on his resume. That army doctor who thought he knew everything had seen to that.

But luckily, or at least so he thought at the time, just a few weeks after he came home in disgrace, he met the woman who would become his wife. So petite, with all that shiny black hair. It seemed like she always dressed in kid's clothes, she was so tiny, and she looked so young, which, actually, she was. After all, he had married her when she was just seventeen. She still had a whole year of high school to finish.

Before they got married, she always listened to him. She never told him what to do, and she did not seem to care about his lack of higher education. Once he got that equivalency, he thought he had it made.

But she never, not for one minute, stopped reminding him that he couldn't get the good jobs because he hadn't gone to college. And since he never wanted to work on his daddy's farm, he needed a job.

He had several jobs, that was for sure, but none of them was right for him. The bosses were all dopes and the work was boring, meaningless, and humiliating. And that last one had cost him, big time.

They were now nearly at the main road, the one that would lead to the highway, and eventually to the rest stop where they would get their next car. Off to the right, his headlights picked up the reflection from a car parked near a small house. It was pretty isolated out here, and in just a few minutes, he had the license plates of that car in his back seat.

Then they were on the road again. He would be sure to steal an American car this time.

Karl double-checked the area to make sure no other cars were nearby before he pulled into the parking space next to the gold Ford Taurus wagon. He had seen a million of them since they got to Illinois, cookie-cutter cars for cookie-cutter people, and he hoped it would be as invisible as that Volvo wagon had been. It was too bad that he could not get this one the same way that he got that one, with the key and without having to kill anyone. If he was to be absolutely honest, however, the killing part did not bother him all that much.

That had been kind of a surprise, the first time he did it. The feeling, as his knife pierced that boy's flesh, was very strange. But when it happened it was as if he were doing it to someone else, like to that parole officer who thought that it was just possible that maybe he should not be granted parole after all, what with his temper and everything. It would have been a pleasure to stick it to her. Or maybe that army doctor who could have given him an honorable or even just a plain discharge. Would that have been so hard? But no, he had to make it dishonorable, just because Karl had pissed him off. If he was so easily upset he really had no right being a shrink. If Dr. Headshrinker only knew what Karl was up to now, he would be scared all right.

Killing that boy, and then those others, had been okay substitutes for some of the people Karl hated. And what did it mean in the great scheme of things, anyway? It just meant a few less stupid people in the world.

It was not so good, though, when his little girl was there to watch him kill someone, but he did not have time, or a place, to stash her. And he still wasn't real sure that she would cooperate even if he did.

That was why they were going to where he had planned. No one would bother them. Not by the time they got there. By November twenty-first it was empty. It would stay that way for weeks probably, or at least long enough.

A Pontiac drove slowly past them, and looked like it was searching for something. It might have been an unmarked car, or someone also trying to stay out of sight. Karl tried to think of what he would do if the car parked nearby. His skin prickled uncomfortably. He could not take a chance that he might get caught by the person in the Pontiac while he took care of the Taurus's owner.

Why was the Pontiac driving so slowly? Why didn't the driver either park or get out of there? Karl put his fingers over the keys of the Camry, ready to start the engine and leave. He would have to find another car. Better safe than sorry.

But after a few seconds it was clear that the driver was just going slowly over to the gas pumps while consulting a map. Karl exhaled sharply.

The Taurus looked good. It was probably a woman's car, some woman like his ex-wife. It was hard to believe it, but somehow she had found someone to marry her after he gave her the divorce. Well, maybe "gave" was the wrong word. She had blackmailed him for it, with her promise not to press charges for those times when he had to discipline her, as if she had any right to press charges for what a man had to do to his wife to make her behave. With the divorce she had also made him surrender his rights to see his daughter. That man she married had adopted his little girl. It made him so mad he could barely see. They would pay though, he promised himself. They could count on it.

There was nothing to do right now but wait. He looked over at her, and knew that she knew what he was about to do. "Don't say nothing while I take care of this business, you hear?" She nodded. That was about all she could do, since her hands were bound at the wrists, and her ankles were tied. She also had a gag in her mouth, just in case, which was why all she could do was nod. He reached over and pushed her bangs away from her eyes.

Someone was coming toward the Taurus, only it was not a woman. It was a man, a big one, coattails flapping in the breeze, carrying a briefcase. The man also carried a little bag, most likely full of coffee to keep him awake.

He wondered what was so important in the man's brief-case that he did not just lock it in the car instead of carrying

it with him. But Karl did not have much more than a second
to think about it, because it was time to make his move.
With the dome light turned off and the key out of the ignition so it wouldn't make that annoying chime, he slowly
opened the door.

As quietly as he could, he crept around the back of the
Camry and came up behind the man, just as he put his key
into the lock. Since it would be so much easier to push the
knife into the man's heart through the opening of his coat
in the front, instead of through the man's coat and into his
back, he started to spin him around.

But the man was not so easy to spin. And suddenly he
had a gun in his hand, pulled out of the briefcase, which
yawned open, its contents spilling all over the ground.

"Stand back," he said, aiming the gun at his attacker.

Karl put his hands up and dropped his knife. There
seemed to be little he could do, and he tried to think fast.
This was not what he had planned on. He felt beads of
sweat prickle on his forehead and under his sweater.

"What are you trying to do?" the man with the gun
asked. His tone was menacing, but there was a good mea-
sure of fear thrown in. The shaking of the gun emphasized
that.

"I'm sorry," Karl answered, trying to sound innocent. "I
thought you were the guy who's been fooling around with
my wife."

That seemed to stop the man. He opened his mouth, as
if to answer, and then got distracted by the bound-up girl
in the Camry. As he was about to ask about her, he got
shot through the heart by the gun that had been concealed
under his attacker's sweater.

It paid to be prepared.

"I hate using guns," Karl said, picking up his knife and
racing back to the Camry. "They are just too damned
noisy." He started the car and pulled out quickly, but not
so fast that he might draw attention to himself. They drove

around the man's body, with its white shirt all stained in
the front and its uncomprehending eyes staring up at the
sky.

"I didn't know you had a gun," she said, when he removed the gag with his right hand, while his left hand
steered them deftly along the entrance ramp.

He was surprised to hear it. The first words she spoke to
him, and they were "I didn't know you had a gun." Well,
at least it was something. But her voice, which he hadn't
really listened to during the times he had talked to her outside her school, had not been what he expected, even ac-
counting for her nervousness. She had that stupid New
Jersey accent that annoyed him so much while he was living there and waiting for his chance to get her. Not what
he had expected at all.

He couldn't worry about that, though, because he still
needed a car. It was time to put "plan B" into action.

The 11:00 news upset Wally. When she turned it off, she
noticed that Sammy seemed restless. Lonely too. "I'm sorry
there aren't any kids for you to play with," Wally said to
the dog. "It's just us old fogies."

"Speak for yourself," Nate said, reaching out for his
wife. "I like it fine with just the two of us. Especially at
night, when we can be cozy together."

"Ah," Wally said. They had certainly been closer since
the house was empty. Her relationship with Nate was
deeply, deeply satisfying, to the very core of her being,
more so than she could ever have imagined. But she was
still annoyed at his put-down of her attempts to help find
Lori. He had in no way atoned for his sins. "Then take the
dog for a walk so we can go to sleep."

"Sleep?"

"Sleep."

Chapter Seventeen

Elliot called Dominique with the information that old Mrs. Bristol, the school secretary, who proved that real relics never change, had given him. "His name is Karl Dickens. Last known address was Riverbend, Nebraska."

Dominique gasped. "Nebraska? It looks like Mrs. Morris was right. I'm on it."

By the time Elliot got to his desk, after driving the three blocks from the school, his partner had a full legal pad of information on their man. She held up her hand to Elliot. "Can you get us a picture?" she said into the telephone. As she reached over and hit the speaker phone button, she put the handset into its cradle.

"It might take a little while," the Midwesterner on the other end said. "But I'll see what I can dig up."

"Sheriff," Dominique said, "my partner just arrived. Can you fill him in?"

"From what I've heard about this guy you're looking for, he could be your man," the sheriff said. "Karl Dickens is bad news. He's been in trouble on and off since he was barely into his teens. Of course, in those days, it was for little things. As he got bigger, I guess, so did his troubles. He even got thrown out of the army. I always thought that little wife of his would straighten him out, especially after they had the baby girl, and I think she did have him on the straight and narrow, at least for a while. But it didn't last, and he got sent to prison. And now we have him listed as a no-show on parole."

"What did he do?" Elliot asked.

"He killed a kid, a little boy. Involuntary manslaughter, they said. I don't know exactly, because it didn't happen here. Still, I read the report. It could've been an accident."

Dominique's long fingers gripped her pencil as she scribbled all the information down. "So he went to jail?"

"He sure did," the sheriff said. "Around here people don't kill other people and not pay for it. I hear that's the way it is in your neck of the woods, but not us. We put 'em away where they belong."

Elliot saw Dominique make a face. Her part of the world had been insulted. Too bad it was often true. To appease her, though, he said into the speaker, "We catch them, but sometimes the juries let them go. Maybe people up here are too used to murder."

The sheriff chuckled. "We all have our problems. Listen, I'll get all of the records we have and send them out to you. We got a fax machine, just like the big police departments, and we'll put it right on."

"Thanks," Dominique said. "We'll call you and let you know if this is the guy."

It had been another long night. They were back in the woods, way off the main road, and she was acting scared. Karl had gotten her back over a week ago, but she did not show any signs yet of the love she used to have for her old dad.

He laughed to himself. She was such a scamp then. She used to run through the house with absolutely nothing on, not a stitch, and never seemed one bit embarrassed in front of him. But now, in the motel rooms, she had kept herself completely covered, even when she was washing out her clothes and waiting for them to dry.

Well, no matter. He was a good father, even if he had not seen his little girl in ten years. That wasn't his fault. Sure, the prison shrink said that he was responsible for all the bad things that happened to him, that he couldn't blame his misfortune on anyone but himself, but what did he know? It was all her fault, his ex's, and he would see that she was sorry. He smiled to himself, thinking how sorry she probably was already, since her daughter was gone. And never coming back.

This whole thing was her doing. From the minute that the accident happened, and that was all it was, as he had sworn a million times, she had kept Jackie away. He never set eyes on her again. A pleasant thought crossed his mind and he couldn't help smiling. Her mother was probably a fat cow by now, turning gray. She would not fit in all those cute little outfits she was always buying for herself when they were married, spending his money. Wasting it was more like it. He snickered a bit to himself. She deserved it. And she deserved to lose Jackie.

He turned on the news whenever he could in those two motel rooms. But there had not been any mention of Jackie's disappearance, although there had been some news of those first two murders. He figured that the police just regarded Jackie as one of those parent kidnapping things, not something to get all excited about. Most policemen just ain't smart. He had proved that often enough as a kid. For every time they caught him, there were five or six other times they did not. They would never in a million years connect Jackie's disappearance with the murders.

He had surprised himself with those. All those years he spent in prison telling himself that he was no murderer, even though Hamlon, the know-it-all cop who arrested him, said he was. He just wouldn't let it alone, no, not that bulldog. He had worried that bone for weeks, pestering Karl and using his huge, towering body to intimidate everyone else who had been there, until he finally had the story. Or at least his version of it. It wasn't Karl's version, that was for sure, but the jury had bought it, and convicted him. And his slimebag drunk of a public defender hadn't done one single thing to get him off. Even so, until last week Karl had been sure that he was no murderer, that it was such an awful thing, and yet, now that he had done it (uh, three times? four?) it didn't seem so hard. Or important. He could even pretend that he was sticking it to Hamlon himself. But that didn't matter right now. What was really important was Jackie.

He would have liked to let her take another shower, would have liked one himself, but they could not go to another motel. Soon they would be at their destination, with hot water to their hearts' content, and a radio, and a TV.

As it got closer to dusk, he began to move. Tonight he would get that car, and they would have everything they needed to get there. Then they could get some of that food he had stocked up on, relax, and get to know one another. What was the word? *Bond.*

The minute the fax came through, Dominique and Elliot drove over to Spot Oil, where Elliot introduced his partner to George. The manager had been busy with a customer, but excused himself to talk to them. "You sure work with some nice looking ladies," he told Elliot.

"Hello, pretty police officer," he said, extending his greasy hand in Dominique direction. She held the faxed picture of Karl Dickens in her right hand so that it was impossible for her to shake hands with George.

He took her avoidance in good spirits. "Do you have something for me?"

She showed him the picture. It was not particularly clear,

or very big, and they knew that it would be difficult for George to make a positive ID, but Elliot held his breath anyway.

"Hm," George said, scratching his head.

They waited while he looked it over, with Elliot losing confidence every second. "It has been several months," the store manager said slowly. "And he only worked here for half of one day."

As Dominique reached for the picture, her disappointment was evident.

"Wait," George said, pulling it back. "Don't be in such a rush, pretty lady. I was going to say, it's been a while, but I'm pretty sure that's him. What's his name again?"

"You have it listed as Richards. But his real name is Dickens."

"Ha! That's funny. He ain't got much of an imagination, I guess."

"I guess not."

"Where'd you get the picture?"

"From his police file. He was out of jail on parole."

"What was he in for? Car theft?"

"No. Manslaughter."

George let out a long low whistle. "Wow."

Dominique nodded. "Right. Wow."

"Listen," George said. "I've been watching the news. They say this guy has killed some other people. What about the girl?"

Elliot spoke up. "We just don't know. Listen, thanks for your time and your help. We have to get back."

George shook his head sadly. "Too bad. Goodbye," he said to Elliot. "And goodbye, pretty lady."

Elliot's muscles were cramped from the hours spent at his desk while he gathered information. He sought unsuccessfully to find a comfortable position for his long legs during one heck of a conversation with the sheriff from the town that was so small it was not on the only map of Nebraska that Elliot could find.

Between the two of them, they established the date when Dickens got out on parole, and spent hours trying to trace his steps after that. Dickens had skipped a meeting with his parole officer less that a week after he got out, which was two and a half months before. Elliot stayed on the phone until he was sure he had as much information as the sheriff. Then he had a good satisfying stretch and went to lunch.

Late in the afternoon he called the Kaufmans and then called Mrs. Morris back with the information he had. She had been such a help that he could not see keeping her in the dark, even though she had a tendency to get on his nerves. Mrs. Morris had all kinds of questions.

"So the police in Nebraska are after him too?"

"Yes. The entire investigation team has been notified. It now includes Nebraska. But they haven't managed to find Dickens either. It looks like we're all on the right track, but we can't seem to catch the train."

"Have you checked with his relatives?" Mrs. Morris asked. "Maybe they know where he is."

"Yes, Ma'am, we called them all. They say they haven't heard from him in years. We also got a copy of all their phone records for the last few months. Most of them live up in Washington state. The rest are in Florida. They haven't heard from him."

"What about his friends?"

"There aren't any that we know of," Elliot said. "At least on the outside. The farm area where the family used to live has all been turned into a mega-farm. None of the old neighbors are around. The neighborhood where the Dickens family lived after Jackie was born is all run-down, practically non-existent. Most of the houses are boarded up, according to the sheriff, with just a few transients in the rest. But the police called the prison and asked some of the men in the cellblock with him if they knew where he might be."

"Did they tell them anything?"

"It was about what you'd expect from cellmates. Most said they'd never tell the cops anything."

"Most?"

"One guy said he had his own little girl, and that he'd never want her or her mother hurt. Apparently his wife is one of the loyal ones. He said that Dickens said he was going to find his little girl. And that he knew where to look, even though her mother had run off with her."

"So Jackie's parents were hiding here?"

"I guess they were trying."

"They're the key," Mrs. Morris said. "We have to get them to tell us where he might have taken Lori. And we have to hope that she hasn't convinced him that she isn't Jackie. It's her only chance."

"They won't talk," Elliot said. "They pulled Jackie out of school as of this morning and they refuse to discuss this."

"Can't you threaten them with obstructing justice or something?"

"We're working on it. It takes time."

He was on the telephone with the police network when Dominique gestured to him that he should leave or he would miss his class. It would not do to miss it again, so he handed her the receiver and bolted out the door.

There it was. Another Taurus. This one was navy. Good enough.

Karl chuckled. He must really have his heart set on a Taurus, he thought. But sometimes you just couldn't get the color you wanted. Oh well.

She was tied up again. "This is the last time we have to do this, sweetheart," he assured her. "I know you wouldn't try to run away from your Dad, but you might be tempted to scream or something while I'm getting us this car. I wouldn't want you to do that. We have to be real quiet."

She blinked. He knew she understood.

This time he was taking no chances. Even though it was kind of cold out—it had been frigid since they entered Iowa—he sat outside the Taurus, right near the rear bumper. He loved it when people backed into parking spaces for no reason. They made such a big deal about getting in, so that they could get out easy, like it saved them effort in the long run. How stupid can people get?

He had watched the whole thing, and he saw the woman who got out. Small. Easy. So he waited.

Chapter Eighteen

Elliot's desk phone rang almost as soon as he sat down. Dominique was not due for another half hour, when their shift officially started. But Elliot had spent a restless, almost sleepless night, due to the fact that with so much happening on this case, there was still not enough.

"Levine," he said into the receiver.

"We have another one." The desk sergeant's voice sent chills down Elliot's spine. He could picture Kennedy sitting in the dispatch center in semi-darkness, vigilantly watching the monitors and scanning the notices as they came in on the network, as he did all day. Twinkling lights on the computer panels and muffled voices all conveyed information from around the country, and the latest was this. They had been expecting another one, but not this soon.

"Iowa this time," Sergeant Kennedy said, in response to Elliot's first question.

"Sounds like he's headed to Nebraska," Elliot said. He fought to keep cool despite the flush that had come over him. *When would this end?*

"I don't know about that," the sergeant said. "According

133

to the reports, this time he was on a north-south road, heading north, maybe to Canada. We could lose him."

"How do they know it's him?"

"That Camry that was missing was abandoned at the scene, after he knifed another lady. This one was the mother of four little kids who had been visiting her ailing mother."

Elliot felt a terrible sense of guilt. He swallowed hard. "What's he driving now?"

"A Taurus wagon."

"Another anonymous car. He'll be harder to find." Elliot jotted down the information, and as Dominique walked in, he pointed to the pad. "Thanks," he said, and hung up. Her face when she saw the message reflected his feelings. *Damn!*

She couldn't believe it. He was telling another one of those stories featuring himself as the star and everyone else as idiots. Lori listened carefully, but silently. She was too afraid to talk, even though she wished she could tell him to shut up.

At first she hadn't understood what was going on. She had been walking home, just like always, when out of nowhere popped this man.

It wasn't the first time she had seen him. He was the same man who once thought she was Jackie. At first it had only seemed a little strange, but this time it was different. He was talking to her as if she, or Jackie, should know him, but he wasn't anyone whom she had ever seen with Jackie, or any of her other friends.

He really didn't pop out of nowhere, she knew. He came out of a blue Volvo wagon. At first she thought he was someone's dad, maybe offering her a lift. But then he started talking weird, like he was her own father!

She tried to tell him she wasn't Jackie. But as soon as she said the word "not," he grabbed her, and put his hand over her mouth. Then she heard another voice asking if she needed help. And right after that, this man stabbed a boy, actually stuck a knife right into him in front of her very eyes!

She had been so stunned that she just went limp. He had stuffed her into the car, and in no time they were driving down the street.

That was when she tried to get away. At the stop sign at the end of the street, she opened the door and got half-way out. But he grabbed her back, making her drop her keys. And he did not even slow down again, even for stop signs, until they were away from the area.

She had not been able to tell where they were going for a few minutes, but suddenly they were on the entrance ramp to I-78, headed west.

She knew she should have tried harder to escape. It was a thought that had crossed her mind many times over the past week. But at the time all she could think about was the boy, bleeding in the bushes, and how she didn't want to end up like that.

So she kept quiet and listened. After about three hours she had it figured out. He thought she was Jackie, and he was Jackie's real father. The one she hardly ever talked about, who had been sent to jail. It was enough to make Lori keep very quiet.

Not talking gave her plenty of time to think. She reasoned out that he thought Jackie was still blond. Those old pictures that Mrs. Gibson kept around were always so funny, because Jackie just didn't look that way anymore. They could have been Lori, Mrs. Gibson always said. Now they were, sort of.

She also knew that if she talked, he might ask her questions and she might not know the answer. What his name was was one of those questions. And she didn't know many stories about their life together.

So she listened while he talked, and learned the stories.

And she was very careful not to let him see her undressed, not just for modesty's sake, but because she didn't have the beauty mark that Jackie had.

She was very aware of the mark. It was the whole reason that the cheerleaders' costumes didn't include cutoff shirts, even for indoor games. Jackie hated the mark and never wore two-piece bathing suits because of it. Lori didn't have it and she couldn't let Jackie's father find out.

Being there was so gross! Disgusting! She couldn't ever use a real bathroom, except for the two times they went to a motel. Not only that, he had kept her tied up for most of the time they were there. Her clothes were so grungy; they were the same ones she had worn all week.

And they only ate cold food and drank soda. She would give anything for fresh food. But he kept saying that when they got to where they were going, things would be better. He had been saying that ever since he kidnapped her.

Since then, he had killed five people! Lori knew he thought that she didn't see the first woman he killed, the one whose car they had for so many days. But she did.

She wasn't really sleeping most of the time he thought she was sleeping, but she had to keep him quiet sometimes, so she pretended to be asleep. When he thought she was asleep, he drummed endlessly on the steering wheel, while his head bopped up and down to some imaginary music.

Whenever he knew she was awake he talked and talked. He answered his own questions, since she wouldn't talk. She knew by these one-sided conversations that he was totally off his rocker. He claimed that he could tell by her eyes how much she still loved him. Only a crazy man would think that fear was love.

She thought about all those people he had attacked. She knew they died. She could just tell. Although she secretly hoped that somehow they had been found in time to be saved, she didn't really believe it. Especially after she saw it mentioned on the news they watched at the motel. And she was sure that if he found out about her, she would be next.

Now he was taking her somewhere, somewhere he said they would never be found. He would probably find out who she really was and that would be the end. And there was absolutely nothing else she could do!

She had tried twice to do something. The first time they stopped she had reached into her jacket for a piece of paper and her silver pen. But she had not had time to write anything before he pulled her out of the car and pushed her into the other one.

Then when they abandoned that car, she tried to write another note. But this time she couldn't find her pen, her favorite, beautiful pen. She didn't know where she lost it. And she couldn't write a note. There was no hope.

She missed her father and her sister. But most of all she missed her mother, and longed to be held by her, safe and sound. Lori fought off the tears that pricked her eyes and made her nose sting. She realized that she might never again see the woman she argued with the most in the world, and would never again have that safe feeling. How would it be if she could never tell her mother that she loved her? What if it was already too late?

After a while, they passed a sign that said WELCOME TO MINNESOTA. It was dark, and the desolate landscape outside the car did not look any different to Lori than the last state had. She couldn't believe that she had been in any of the places that they had gone through, although the hard reality of whom she was with, and what was at stake, was undeniable. She almost laughed to herself. She could believe that she was in a stolen car with a madman murderer who thought she was his daughter, but she could not believe that she had just driven through Iowa.

"It won't be long now," he said. "You won't believe your eyes, but the place looks mighty good now. I wonder if you'll remember it."

I guarantee I won't, thought Lori. *But I am not about to tell you that.*

Mostly, she wished she knew where they were going, so she could prepare herself.

"It hasn't changed much," he said. "But it has improved. It's not rundown like so many of the other ones."

Lori fought the urge to ask "What other ones?"

An hour and a half after they got to Minnesota, the Taurus bumped down a dirt road. Bare trees made scary silhouettes against the darkened sky. There was a three-quarter moon, and Lori could see a lake reflecting the moonlight. It was kind of peaceful, but also sinister.

"Any minute you'll see it," he said. He seemed so excited. His voice quivered, and his hands alternated between gesticulating and grabbing the steering wheel to keep the car moving straight along the deeply rutted road.

They were in the middle of nowhere. It had been at least a half hour since they saw the last lights of civilization. And that had been no more than a small cottage set way back in the woods.

He turned the car precipitously to the right. It looked for a minute like they were going into the trees, but then Lori saw that they were on an even less-traveled road.

This road was in worse condition than the other and was on a sharp incline. They bumped and jolted upward for almost five minutes.

Then they broke into a clearing. It was enormous, and, as they rolled past each small building, Lori could see that they were in a campground. She hadn't seen a sign for it, but she knew this was a summer camp.

They drove slowly over to one of the buildings. "This is it!" he announced. "We're home!"

Chapter Nineteen

As much as she wanted to hear if there were any developments in Lori's case, Wally knew that now was not the time to call Elliot. She was very frustrated.

It was time to do something—anything—constructive. But her mind was too full of everything that was happening. Elliot should have found that man by now. He said that practically the whole country was looking for him. What was taking so long?

Reluctantly, Wally busied herself with cleaning her oven. It would soon be time for Thanksgiving. But she could not help wondering, on behalf of so many people, *thanks for what?*

Lori woke up groggily, completely confused about where she was. After a moment she realized that she was in a bed. A real one, soft and comfortable. She was grateful. When she sniffed, she could smell steam coming up from the faintly hissing radiator. She snuggled down and tried to go back to sleep.

But the familiar fear took over and made her get up. She opened her eyes again and took a look around.

The bedroom she was in was small, way smaller than her own at home. It had a pitched roof that sloped nearly all the way down to where the bed was. Lori figured that was the outer wall. The room was cheerfully furnished with old-fashioned quilts on the walls and bed, and had frilly curtains on the windows and a rag carpet on the floor.

Touching her feet to the chilly floor, she went over to the window and looked out at the cold, bare landscape, while her memory flooded back from the night before.

They had come into the small house at around midnight, and he had reached over, right past her face, to turn on the heat switch. She could hear the rumbling of the furnace as he went around turning on lamps here and there. Then he went into the kitchen and turned on the overhead fluorescent light.

"We'll have to set these out to defrost for breakfast," he said, as he took a container of milk out of the freezer. "Let's have some bacon and eggs too. Sorry, I just have those egg substitute things, because I didn't want to take a chance that they wouldn't be good when we got here. We'll have a good breakfast tomorrow for sure, nice and hot. I'll have some coffee and you can have hot chocolate. Just like the old days."

He looked around the room. "So how does it look? Better than the old days? They winterized it when they renovated, and put that old furnace into working condition, so that they could use it for cross-country ski weekends. But it's too soon for those." He chuckled. "By then . . . Well, they did a good job, didn't they?"

She rubbed her eyes, but did not say anything.

"Oh, you must be tired," he said. "Well, you know where your room is. Go on up, and I'll tuck you in soon."

She froze, her feet felt glued to the linoleum floor. What was he talking about? Her room? Jackie's? Jackie had been here? She had never mentioned this place. What was she going to do? He would know in a second if she made a mistake. Somehow she made her feet move toward the stairs, hoping that possibly she could get away with this. Maybe she could figure out which was hers.

The stairwell was narrow and steep, wallpapered in bright daisies, and she held onto the rail with white-knuckled hands, praying that somehow she would find the right room. At the very least, if she were wrong, maybe he'd just think that she forgot.

But it was not as hard as she thought. There were only two rooms on the second floor, and one was obviously the master bedroom. So she took the other, washed up quickly in the bathroom, and got into bed.

He came in soon after. "You didn't find your pajamas?"

She stared at him.

"I put them in the right drawer, I think. Didn't you look?"

He went over to the dresser and opened the second drawer from the top. He pulled out a long flannel night-gown and a pair of thermal pajamas.

"Which do you want for tonight?" he asked. She did not know what to say. While she wracked her brain to remember what Jackie preferred on sleep-overs, he explained where they came from.

"I bought you all this stuff. Just wait until you see it." He went over to the closet and opened the door. It was packed full of clothes, dresses, skirts, pants and sweaters. "I got you shoes and everything you need."

She could not resist asking. "How?"

"How did I get it here, or how did I know your size?"

Lori nodded. *Answer either*, she thought.

"I bought it all for you after the first time I saw you. I'm pretty sure it'll fit, even the shoes, because I have a good eye for size. Do you remember the year I was a shoe sales-man? I could always spot those old cows who were trying to force their size eight-and-a-half feet into size seven

shoes. That was the year you had sneakers in three colors
and party shoes that fit, even though you kept growing so
fast. I was sure your feet would never stop getting bigger."
He laughed, a harsh, creepy laugh. "And I brought all these
things here when I came back to set the place up before I
got you, so that it would be all ready."

Lori did not say anything.

"Aren't you going to say 'Thank you, Daddy'?"

She could not say anything. Although she tried, nothing
came out.

He seemed to get angry at that. "Or are you like your
mother and you only want to know how much it cost and
where I got the money?" His face had turned into a sneer.

"No."

"I'm sorry sweetheart," he said. "I guess I'm a little tired
too. You go to sleep now, and we'll talk more in the morning."

She waited for him to get the ropes to tie her into bed
like he had done in those motel rooms. But he did not. He
just turned out the light and closed the door.

A few seconds later, though, a key turned in the lock.
And now, the next morning, the door was still locked.

Lori sat back down on the bed feeling the warmth of the
sun coming through the curtains. She wondered if she
would be able to go to the bathroom. It had become a habit
to resist the need for long periods of time because it was
so horrible to go out in the woods, but she was feeling a
lot more comfortable in the house. As prisons go, it was
not so bad, she reflected. But she would like to use the
facilities.

She knocked softly on the door and waited for him to
come. Then she got frightened that he might be angry
again, so she quickly put on the nightgown he had shown
her the previous evening. Soon she heard footsteps on the
stairs.

The key turned in the lock, and he opened the door. "You

look so cute in that," he said, with a big smile on his face. "And see? It fits perfectly. Did you sleep well? That bed is so soft."

She nodded and forced a smile of her own. Then she motioned that she would like to go use the bathroom.

"Plenty of towels in there, and the water is nice and hot. Plenty of soap and all the hair products a girl like you could need to keep that gorgeous blond hair shiny. All the comforts of home." He stood aside for her to pass. "Have a good long one. I'll start breakfast."

Lori stayed in the shower until her fingers looked like prunes. She washed her hair three times and let the conditioner sit on it for five full minutes before rinsing it out. After towel-drying her hair, Lori noticed that there was no hair blower, but decided not to mention it. It might help her live longer.

She used her brand-new toothbrush, and her brand-new comb and put on brand-new clothing, for what was supposed to be her brand-new life.

Then she went downstairs to do something else brand-new. She was going to have to eat bacon. She knew Jackie loved it, but although her family did not keep strictly kosher, she had never tasted it.

But what bothered her most was, then what?

On the national evening news motorists were being warned about rest stops in the Midwest states. The Sunday anchor, a no-nonsense fortyish woman, stated that police in nine states were on the lookout for a man who had stolen several cars from people at rest stops along routes 78, 80, and 90. "Be wary. Be safe," she said. "And that's our news for tonight. Join us tomorrow at six for the breaking stories. Goodnight."

No mention was made of the connection with Lori Kaufman. Wally breathed a sigh of relief. It may just have saved her life.

Chapter Twenty

"We think he's holed up," the voice on the other end of the phone said. It was not what Elliot wanted to hear.

The state police had tracked him for a while in Minnesota, and had a positive ID on him, the girl, and the car, from one of the gas stations. But then he had disappeared. They were certain, however, that he had not gone into Canada, since every border crossing was aware of the situation.

He knew from the reports that the Minnesota state police were interested in this case. That was understandable, since the crime that landed him in jail was committed in Minnesota, where he had served his time. Elliot wondered if that was related somehow to him holing up there.

"Have you checked with the families of any of the inmates he served time with?" he asked the officer. "Maybe he's hiding with someone like that."

"We're checking now. We'll keep you posted." He hung up.

When Dominique came, he told her what the police in Minnesota thought. "It's a large state, tremendous, and he might not even still be in it, but they are searching. I'm afraid it's like looking for a needle in a haystack."

"I wish they had some way to limit this particular haystack. I keep thinking that we're running out of time." She sat down sadly. "I was so hopeful yesterday. After church, I just had this good feeling."

"We have to find a way to figure out where he could be hiding."

"What makes you think we can figure out something that police in nine states and the FBI can't figure out?"

"Now who's down?" Elliot asked.

Wally patted the frozen but fully-cooked brisket she was bringing to the Kaufman family. She also had a package of noodles that could be boiled and some broccoli and a loaf of fresh rye bread from the bakery. They would be a good way to start talking. She had an idea that maybe, since Jackie's family was still refusing to cooperate, she could find out more from Lori herself. And if it really worked the way she had been told, there was only one way to do that.

Sandy invited her right in. Wally explained the cooking instructions, and assured Sandy that she could take her time in returning the microwaveable dish.

Taking a good look at Sandy, Wally saw that she was very pale, and thinner, about what could be expected. Her eyes had developed raccoon rings. It was enough to break Wally's heart.

She poured herself a cup of coffee at Sandy's suggestion and sat at the kitchen table, across from her. "All those murders," Sandy said. "And Lori is right in the middle of it."

Wally nodded. "He thinks she is his daughter, so he won't hurt her."

"What if he sees it on the news that it's Lori Kaufman who's missing, not Jackie?"

"It hasn't made the national news, not the part about her. And as long as they don't announce the connection between Lori and the murders at the rest stops, he won't figure it out."

Sandy did not look appeased. "Are you sure?"

"Yes." Wally was not sure at all. She could be totally wrong. Yet the fingerprints they had found in that poor woman's Camry had been identified as Jackie's real father's. It was a strong indication that the working theory had some validity.

"But do you think he's feeding her properly?" Sandy asked. "And what is she wearing? She only left with the clothes on her back. She's not the type to rough it, you know. We sent her to a luxury summer camp one time, and she practically made us take her home after she saw a spider in the shower."

"She's probably a little tougher now. Have you seen the showers in the locker room at the high school? If she could take one there, she can survive anywhere."

Sandy looked at Wally as if wondering if she were serious. Then she laughed. "I guess you're right about that. I have seen them. They're disgusting."

Both women were quiet for a few minutes.

"Everyone is being so nice," Sandy said. "Patty McDermott came over a while ago with some things for Felice that her daughter made. Do you know her?"

Wally nodded.

Sandy continued softly, with a catch in her voice. "Patty said that they said a prayer for Lori in church yesterday."

"That was nice of Patty's family," Wally said.

Sandy shook her head. "It was, but it isn't why I'm telling you about it. As I understand it, the pastor said a prayer out loud. And Patty said that Jackie started to cry and her parents stood up in the middle of everything and took her out of the church. Patty said that Jackie's mother looked angry. But Jackie can't help the way that she feels. I understand it. We're all helpless."

"We have to try to help. We can't leave it all up to the police," Wally said.

There was pain and frustration in Sandy's eyes that was almost too much for Wally to bear. But she straightened her back and let out a gush of air. "What can we do?"

"We can try to be smart about this, and see if we can figure it out." Wally did not want to add that if Jackie or her mother would only open their mouths the whole thing could be over with. That was for the courts to decide, and the papers had been filed. Until they got around to it, however, she and Sandy could not just sit there.

Wally had to ask. "I know this sounds strange," she said, cautiously, "but would it be possible for me to see Lori's diary? You got it back from Elliot, didn't you?"

"Yes," Sandy said, her voice coming in a sigh. "Why?"

"I just thought that maybe she mentioned something, like more than that incident of the man thinking she was Jackie."

"Do you think it's important? The police had the diary for two days, and I'm sure they went through it."

Wally was sure of that too, and that she probably would not find anything. But then she had another idea. "Has Lori been keeping diaries for long?"

Sandy seemed to be trying to remember. "Since fifth or sixth grade, I think. Why?"

"It may sound silly, but maybe she wrote something down about Jackie that could help. Let's see. They met in ninth grade, right? Maybe you could let me see the ones from then on."

Sandy did not say anything. Her eyes clouded over.

Wally was not even sure she was on the right track but she felt she had to try. "I'd bring them back tomorrow" was all she could think of to say.

"Well," Sandy said. "I guess it's okay." She left the room and returned with the diaries a few minutes later. "Please take care of them. The police got some dirt on the one they took." She frowned. "Lori is going to be so mad that I let anyone see it." She started to cry. "If she finds out."

Wally stood up very straight, and, fighting the prickling tears in her own eyes, said, "She will, and we'll have to be very brave when we tell her we snooped." She watched Sandy's face when she said that, and they both laughed the way the mothers of teenagers must, with lumps in their throats and fear in their hearts.

He fiddled around with the television set for an hour. All he got was snow. Then he set to work on the radio. After a while, and some swearing, he was able to get a station to come in clearly. A few minutes later, Lori realized that it was only farm news and weather. Light snow was forecast.

Lori sat watching him, unable to get herself to speak. She could not think of one single thing to say that would not eventually give her away.

There was nothing else to do, however. She had stopped fantasizing a few days back that someone might rescue her. Certainly not Hull Jackson. As cute as he was, he probably had not even noticed she was missing yet. It made her feel silly for a second, when she thought about that ridiculous crush she'd had on him, but at this point that did not really matter. Nothing did. She was stuck here with a maniac and no one would ever find her.

It was nice enough in the house. She looked around the room at the brightly flowered chintz sofas and the ceramic animals near the fireplace. The house was furnished in a kind of rustic garden motif, not Lori's taste, but certainly better than the interior of a stolen car. The last one, the one that was parked outside, had been full of toys and used teething pretzels. Lori could not bear to think of the baby who had lost its mother.

She looked beyond the living room, through the windows, to the cabins and other buildings of the camp. They were also well-kept and newly painted, with carpets of leaves and pine needles around them. Looking at the worn paths that led away from the cabins, she wondered where they went.

"I can't get anything on this damn radio," he said. "And the TV is worthless. I'm going to have to get us a satellite dish."

He turned to her. "I'm sorry I forgot your tapes," he said. "I should have taken them out of the car."

Lori remembered those tapes. He had played *Peter and the Wolf, The Nutcracker, Peter, Paul and Mommy,* and *Carnival of the Animals* before they got to Allentown. In the back of her mind, she vaguely remembered that Jackie had said she liked that kind of stuff, so she did not question why he kept playing them.

Finally she was able to say something. "Can I go for a walk?"

"Good idea," he said, jumping to his feet. "I'll go with you. I knew you'd want to see the old place."

Damn! That wasn't what she had in mind. But she had to get some air.

She went to get her coat from the closet next to the front door.

It seemed to take forever for Wally to do the rest of the things she had to do that day, and it was not until after the dinner dishes were done that she had a chance to look at the diaries. She made herself a hot cup of Earl Grey tea and sat down in her favorite reading chair near a strong light. More than anything, she hoped she could find a clue to Lori's whereabouts, but she had no idea if she would even know it if she saw it. Hopefully, she thought, as she took a sip of her tea, she would find what she needed.

It really was embarrassing to see the way the mind of a high school girl worked. The only thing worse, Wally reflected, would have been to actually be a high school girl again. Or adolescent any age, for that matter. The very idea made her skin prickle.

Aside from Lori's hopes and fears for every nuance of conversation between her and that boy, Hull, Lori seemed most recently to still be in the stage of wavering between hating her life and her family and loving them so much that she could not bear the thought of leaving for college. She could not wait to go, she was sure she was an adult already, and she did not see how she could compete with all those sophisticated kids from other high schools who were so much smarter and prettier and better at everything. The only thing she felt confident about was her cheerleading, in which she considered herself superior to all others, except of course Jackie, whom she considered her equal.

While she read, it became clear to Wally that Lori envied Jackie and felt sorry for her at the same time. She thought Jackie's mother was much cooler than her own, younger and more with it, which was typical, although she seemed bothered by the fact that Mrs. Gibson was very strict and insisted that Jackie have an early curfew.

Wally knew the routine. She had two daughters of her own, after all, and she knew many other women in the same boat. The mothers she knew had been comparing notes about raising daughters since the little girls started playgroup. All the girls were about the same. They each had their special talents, to be sure, and some had nicer personalities than others, but they pretty much all felt the same way about their families until that magical day when they went off to college.

One thing caught Wally's eye in one of the earlier diaries. It seemed that Lori was aware that Jackie was not living with, and did not see, her biological father. *That is a relief*, thought Wally. *Maybe Lori knew enough to play along.*

Lori had asked how it felt not seeing her real dad, and Jackie had surprised her by saying it was fine. *She said,* wrote Lori, *that the only time she liked him was when they were away for summer vacation every year. I don't under- stand why Jackie's father had to work on their vacation, but she said he was mostly nicer during that time than home. When they were home,* Lori wrote a few lines later, saying it sounded awful, like a farm, *and no TV!!!!!* she said Jackie had told her *he was mean to her and to her mother. And when he was sent to jail, she decided never to speak to him again. And she said she never did.* Lori had thought that amazing. She wrote, *I can't imagine hat- ing Dad like that, or never seeing him.*

Wally felt that she had a clue. She took a sip of tea, but found, to her great disappointment, that it was stone cold.

"Bleh." Putting her cup down quickly, her first inclina- tion was to call Elliot, but she thought he was probably at his class. So she kept it to herself, and tried to think of what she could do to help. She looked at her watch, and seeing the time, headed off to bed, where Nate, the great skeptic who told her she was wasting her time, was already asleep.

It was one of those nights when she just couldn't fall asleep. She had too much unfinished business.

Karl could not sleep. Here he was, home free, and he could not relax. His little girl was in the room right next door, and yet he could not feel close to her. Maybe it was because she was locked in, like he didn't trust her or some- thing. That was really wrong, and he knew it, but he just could not take a chance.

Where would she go, anyway? he wondered. They were miles from anywhere, and she would not remember how to get to town. In fact she had seemed to remember very little about this place. Sure, she knew where her room had been, but not much else. It was funny how her mind worked.

The worst part was that she still was not talking. *She should be talking by now*, he thought, and it was getting on his nerves. Sometimes her mother would not talk to him for days at a time, and that really made him mad. She had better not try that stuff on him. He did not want any reminders of that woman.

Chapter Twenty-one

Wally awoke with the premonition that time was running out. It was still twenty minutes before the alarm, but she jumped up and shook Nate out of his slumber. "I have to go out," she whispered into his ear. He nodded, without opening his eyes, and turned over. She quickly showered and dressed and went to leave him a note, because she was sure he would never remember that she told him she was leaving. She was actually grateful that he hadn't awakened, because he undoubtedly would have tried to talk her out of going on her mission.

After writing it out hastily she put the note on the refrigerator. He would have no trouble seeing it now that the front of the fridge was clear. Ever since Mark graduated, they had few notices to put on it.

She had to try to talk to Jackie. There was no doubt in her mind that the girl could provide a clue, and they needed a lead quickly. She was even more certain that Jackie's mother would have a good idea of where to find her ex-husband, but it was unlikely that she could convince Mrs. Gibson to talk to her.

Although Wally was sure it was necessary, approaching Jackie would be difficult. It was reported that she had not been going to school, and Wally suspected that she hadn't been going out of the house at all. The family would not accept phone calls from outsiders, according to the newspaper, and Wally had no relationship with the family to get to talk to Jackie.

All of that aside, she had to try.

After a few minutes of driving around, uncertain where to go, she made a decision. It might not work, but she headed her car over to Sandy's house.

When she got there she noticed that it was an even worse mess than the day before, strewn with trash left by the ever-present media. Apparently, someone had been cleaning it up a little, maybe for the thrice-daily film crews, because the center of the steps and the bushes closest to them were cleared of debris. But beyond that small area, it looked like a dump. It was shameful.

Sandy greeted her at the door and smiled groggily. Her face was more relaxed, probably owing to the fact that it had not fully awakened, and she looked a bit like her old self. But it did not last long, and as she pulled herself together to talk to Wally, her worry lines reappeared. "Good morning," she said. "You're out early."

Wally stammered, "Er, yes." She did not ordinarily drop in on people at 7:30 in the morning. Hopefully, though, she would be forgiven.

"Why don't you come in for some coffee?" Sandy asked. "I just put it on. Jeff is leaving for the office. His business can't survive all this neglect."

A cup of coffee would be useful, Wally thought, since she had not had anything to eat yet. She followed Sandy to the kitchen, where the aroma of the freshly-brewed coffee and the noise of the coffee maker filled the room.

"Just put your coat on a chair," Sandy said, as she got down two mugs. She set a milk carton on the table, one with a picture of a missing girl on the side, and grimaced at it. "I'm too tired to put the milk in a pitcher. I haven't been sleeping well."

Wally poured some milk into her coffee and stirred thoughtfully.

"I can't thank you enough for that brisket," Sandy said. "It was as good as my mother used to make. I can never seem to make it that way. Usually no one here will eat it. Maybe you could give me the recipe?" She stopped, seeming to have run out of steam. "For when Lori comes home," she added quietly.

"I'd love to," Wally said. She was almost afraid to make her request but forced herself. "Now, I wonder if you'd do something for me?"

"What?" Sandy asked, with the look of a woman who has no idea how she could do anything for anyone, considering.

"Could you try to get Jackie on the phone? I'd like to talk to her, privately, and I don't know how. But maybe they'll let you talk to her."

Sandy did not ask why, although she seemed to know. It was a relief to Wally. She hated to get Sandy's hopes up, especially if it turned out that it wouldn't help find Lori.

"I could use her private number," Sandy said. "Her mother might not be watching that one, because only Jackie's friends have it."

"Great," Wally said. She watched Sandy dial the number, and listened as she talked to Jackie. But mostly she went over in her mind what she would say to the girl.

"I'd like you to talk to someone," Sandy was saying. "She is trying to help. Please listen to her." She paused. "For Lori."

Wally took the receiver from Sandy's shaking hand. "Hello," she said, tentatively. "I'm Wally Morris, uh, Mark's mother." She was not even sure that Jackie knew Mark, but had no idea how else to explain who she was.

"What do you want from me?" Jackie asked. "I already talked to the police."

"They needed to know about you," Wally said carefully. "They think that maybe Lori was mistaken for you."

Jackie did not speak. Wally knew that what she had said to the girl was not news, and that she had probably been badgered about it already by more than just the news media, but she continued. "That might put you in danger," she said. "Your mother and father would worry."

"Then you should talk to them," Jackie said angrily. "My mother doesn't want me to tell anyone."

"That's because she wants to protect you. I can understand that. Lori is not her priority. But I thought you might like to help her. She really needs it."

Jackie began to sniffle. "I'd like to help," she cried. "But I don't know how."

Wally thought hard about her nursery school teacher training, and how to get a child to open up. Her hand on the phone receiver was sweating, but she held it steady as she chose her words carefully. "You know that the police think that the kidnapper may have been after you, don't you?"

"Yes, but I don't know if that's true. Maybe it is. What do you need to know?"

"I want to know about your father. Mr. Gibson isn't your biological dad, is that right?"

"Yes. But he's the best father in the world!"

"I'm sure he is. But I want to ask you about your father, Karl Dickens."

There was silence on the other end of the line. Wally was afraid that the girl would hang up. She held her breath.

"I could get in trouble for talking to you," Jackie said quietly, after a long pause. "My mother told me that I should never talk about him."

"It might help Lori," Wally said. "I know you want to help her, don't you?"

"Yes, but how could it help? He doesn't know her. How could he?"

Wally could hear tears in Jackie's voice. "I'm not sure that it can help," Wally said. "But I want to try." She took a deep breath. "I know you haven't seen him in many years. He doesn't know what you look like now, does he?"

"He did a terrible thing, and I don't want to see him. He and my mom got divorced."

"I know. He gave up custody of you, didn't he?"

"Yes," Jackie said, with a tight voice. "I think he still wanted me, but Mom told him if he gave me up she wouldn't press those other charges."

Wally wondered what they were, but did not want to ask. Not now, at least.

"I have to tell you something," she said instead. "I read Lori's diary. Actually, several of her diaries. In one she talked about you and your father. She said that you didn't like him, except for when you were at a vacation place. Where is that?"

"How could it matter?" Jackie asked, with her voice raised.

"It might. Where is it?"

"I'm not even sure. It was some place we used to go to in the summer. It took a long time to get there from our house. He had a job there, I think. But he got into trouble after that." She was quiet again. "Then he went to jail and we never went back."

"Your mother would know, wouldn't she?" Wally asked.

"She won't talk to you or anyone. She doesn't want to even think about my dad."

"But maybe she could help," Wally said, in frustration.

Jackie was silent.

"I'm pretty sure he cares about you, and he did this out of his own form of love," Wally said soothingly.

Jackie's voice was tight. "Why would you think that?"

"Because he brought things that he thought you'd like,"

Wally said, taking a shot in the dark. "He brought your favorite tapes, at least ones he knew you used to like."

"He did?"

"Yes, he had *Peter and the Wolf, The Nutcracker, Carnival of the Animals,* and one other. Now what was it? Oh, I remember: *Peter, Paul and Mommy.*"

"How do you know?" Jackie asked, a little breathlessly.

"He left them behind in one of the cars." As soon as she said that, Wally knew that Jackie would freeze up. She could have kicked herself.

Jackie's voice was cold. "I have to hang up. Someone is coming."

"Please don't . . ." Wally heard a click. Her opportunity was gone, and after what she'd said, she would never have another one.

"Did she tell you anything?" Sandy asked. She looked so hopeful that Wally hated to tell her she still did not have a clue.

"Not really. I don't think she knows anything."

"Oh."

"Look, don't give up hope," Wally said. "We can't do that."

Sandy's eyes filled with tears and she reached for the tissue box on the counter. "I suppose you're right, but . . ."

Wally finished her coffee, put the cup in the sink and picked up her coat. "Hang in there. I'll check on you tomorrow."

All the way to the nursery school she tried to get over the anger she felt with herself. If only she hadn't mentioned the stolen car. She was certain that Jackie could have helped. But now her hopes were gone.

Late in the afternoon, Lori stepped out of the shower feeling warm and relaxed. She reached for the bath towel. Her hair was streaming with water, and she had to take a corner of the towel she had wrapped around her middle to dry her eyes so she could see.

What she saw vaguely reflected in the steamy mirror gripped her with fear. He was standing in the doorway of the bathroom, staring at her.

"Oh my God!" she said, in a hoarse whisper.

"I was just walking by and I got worried." He didn't sound worried, though. His voice was cold and his words measured. "The water had been on for such a long time, and I couldn't tell if you were alive or if you had drowned." His blue eyes glittered like ice and seemed to be boring through the towel.

"I like long showers," she said, trying to sound like a sullen teenager. But she was afraid that he had seen her before she covered her body.

Act natural, she told herself. Putting out her chin, she said, "Knock next time. I'm entitled to my privacy."

"You're entitled to nothing, do you hear?"

Lori did not respond, just pushed past him to get to her bedroom. Ordinarily, if her parents made her mad, she would slam the door. But now she could only manage to close it firmly, and wish there was a key on the inside.

For several minutes Lori sat huddled on the bed, afraid that he might try to come in. If he knew that she was not Jackie, she could kiss her life goodbye.

She had to escape.

It was the mailman's day off, and a temporary carrier mistakenly delivered the mail for the office to the house. Wally sorted through it all, still miserable about her failure to get what she was convinced was crucial information from Jackie. She was too restless to relax, so she brought the mail up to the barn.

Mary Jane took it from her gratefully. "I was running out of things to do. I'm glad you brought this."

Wally looked around approvingly. "You're getting to be

too efficient. You'll be able to run your own agency soon."

"Hm." Mary Jane's smile faded into a puzzled frown. "Maybe not yet. There are still things for me to learn. Here's something I haven't seen before." She held a sample brochure in her hand, but Wally was unable to see what it was about.

"What is it?"

"Something called vacation insurance. What's it for?"

"Oh," Wally said, absently. "It's for people who are going on a vacation but are afraid it will either be canceled, and the tickets are non-refundable, or maybe that it will be rained out, or something like that. Sometimes people with time shares or summer homes that they go to every year will buy it. They want some kind of insurance in case the weather is terrible while they're there and they have to find something to do other than sit on a beach."

"I see," Mary Jane said. "I wonder if people buy it who run camps, in case they have to take the kids to movies or bowling every day. When I was a kid, we had one summer like that."

"It would be a good idea. Maybe they do. If not, maybe Nate should try to sell some." She turned to leave. "Tell him I'll see him later."

As she walked back to the house, she thought of camp. Her kids had gone every summer, and they always liked it. But there were summers when it had rained an awful lot.

Something about it reminded her of what Jackie had said. Without even thinking about it she found herself on the phone to Elliot as soon as she walked into the house.

He answered the phone on the third ring. "Levine."

"This is Wally Morris," she said, without her usual preliminaries. I was wondering about something. What exactly was Dickens in jail for?"

"Uh, um, hold on a sec." Wally heard the sound of the phone receiver being put down and papers being shuffled.

When Elliot came back on the line, he sounded like he

was reading something. "He was convicted of manslaughter."

"I knew that. But what I need to know is when and where."

"Why do you want to know?"

"I'll tell you in a minute," Wally said impatiently. "Just give me the information."

"Okay." The sound of pages of a notebook being flipped came through the phone. "He was charged with throwing a child, a non-swimmer, into a lake, causing the boy to drown. His defense was that he was convinced that the boy would swim if he had to."

Wally could barely get the word out. "Where?"

"In a summer camp in Minnesota. Hm. That was the last state where we had him ID'd. Now will you tell me why you want to know this?"

"I think that may be where he took Lori," Wally said.

"Why would you think it was there?"

"Because Jackie said it was the only place that she and her father were ever happy."

"You talked to Jackie Gibson?"

"Well, yes."

"And she told you about this place?"

"Sort of. I had figured part of it out from an old diary of Lori's, and Jackie kind of confirmed some of it, before she hung up on me."

"This is incredible. I want to hear more about how you did that, but right now I think we'd better check out that camp."

"Right. I'd guess it would be abandoned now, since it's nearly winter. Maybe we can go look."

"I'll take care of it," Elliot said, excitement coming right through the phone. "You stay put. I'll call as soon as I know anything."

* * *

Karl felt his blood start to boil, rising from his toes and ready to burst his head. He had not been this angry in a long time. The prison psychiatrist would have said that he should realize that he was angry with himself, not someone else, and that he should give himself a break and not take it so hard. Everyone makes mistakes.

But this was a monumental mistake. He had wondered at first, and then suspected that something was wrong, but now he was sure. She did not have the chocolate mark. She was not Jackie.

Who was she?

Chapter Twenty-two

The call was logged in at 11:58 A.M. Central standard Time. After listening for a few minutes, the new operator did not know who to put on it, but she consulted with the desk sergeant, and was instructed to immediately ring the appropriate party's extension.

"Hamlon." The person on the other end of the line spoke so loudly and quickly that Hamlon had to hold the phone away from his ear. As he did, he looked around to see who was watching, but saw the desk sergeant gesturing toward his co-workers, with their alarmed and guilty faces. "Slow down, would you?" he asked into the phone. "I can't understand what you're saying."

"Sorry," said the voice of the man, who identified himself as Levine, a detective from somewhere called Gross Vennor, New Jersey. Hamlon listened as Levine repeated his problem, feeling a shiver run down his spine. He jotted down some notes and the return phone number, and as calmly as he could, promised to get back to Levine as soon as possible. After hanging up the phone, he jumped to his feet, surprising even himself at how fast he could move his huge body.

"Karl Dickens?" he bellowed. Several of the older officers scurried away from him, leaving only the desk sergeant
to deal with his rage. "How long have you known about
this?"

"It came up while you were on vacation. You told us not
to disturb you under any circumstances."

Hamlon struggled to get his anger under control. "Why
wasn't I told the minute I came back yesterday?"

"We, uh, we didn't think he was coming this way."

"You people never think this guy is important! If it
wasn't for me, he wouldn't even have been arrested." He
shoved his chair back into the desk and started to run for
the file room. "Swanson," he called to the file clerk, who
met him halfway, "get me that Dickens file now!"

"What's this all about?" Wright asked, a new African-
American officer who was giving some of the older, more
complacent officers a run for their money.

"You weren't here then," Hamlon said, between clenched
teeth. He took a second to calm himself as he sat back
down and began to clear his desk in anticipation of the file.
"About two years after I came on the force, there was this
kid, Travis Donaldson, who died at that summer camp up
near Eagle Point."

"What happened?"

"These geniuses," Hamlon said, in a deliberately loud
and sarcastic voice, "didn't even have an inkling that there
may have been more to the accident than meets the eye.
Not until this guy, a meek little delivery man named Ray-
mond Perry, who had been in the area that day, comes into
the police station to say that it's been bothering him for
months how the kids are treated in the camp. He wonders
how their parents, who pay buckets of money for their kid-
dies to have a good time in the summer, would feel if they
knew.

"So these big shots in here are so busy that no one pays
any attention to Mr. Perry. In fact, some loudmouth starts

tittering that the man is just jealous of those people who have the money to send their little darlings to summer camp. Or that maybe he envies those camp owners who get to take the money from parents while providing a minimum in the way of amenities and cuisine. But this Perry guy is persistent, and follows several of the officers around with his words practically running together, as he tries to get someone to listen. It was so pathetic that finally I took him over to my desk. I felt kind of sorry for him and he seemed to be sincere. I figured that if I at least pretended to care, the man would feel better." Hamlon thought about how the guy seemed to perk up when he sat him down and handed him a cup of coffee.

Wright wheeled his desk chair closer to Hamlon's. "So then what happened?"

"As evidence to support his sense that the children were being mistreated, Mr. Perry gave details of how one of the counselors handled one of the kids. He said that on August third he was delivering fuel to the camp—he'd worked for Great Lakes fuel for something like twelve years at that time—and he saw this man in a bathing suit with a whistle around his neck, and a little boy. The man was yelling at the boy that he must learn to swim or he had better damn well die trying."

Wright blinked. "Who said that?"

"Mr. Perry said that Dickens, or at least the counselor who turned out to be Dickens, said it. He said that the counselor said outright that he did not want any failures on his record. The little boy was bawling his eyes out, saying how he was too scared and he couldn't do it, but no one came to help him, because they were behind the canteen, and no one could hear them over the sound of the tanks being filled." Hamlon wadded up an old sheet of paper from his legal pad and tossed it into the garbage can beside Wright's desk.

"Two points," Wright said. "Then what?"

"So this Perry wants to lodge a complaint with the camp, but he thinks it isn't his place. He can't get it off his conscience, though, for months, and he finally decides that the next time he comes up this way he'll say something, to the camp manager, but by then the camp is already closed for the season. So he comes to the police station as a second choice. He figured we would know what to do. Most of us," Hamlon raised his voice again, "ignored him." Hamlon looked at his watch. "Swanson! What the hell is taking you so long?"

"It isn't here."

"Where the hell is it?"

"I'm checking."

"Do it fast or I'll——"

"Take it easy," Wright said. "He'll get it. So what happened with this Perry guy?"

"I got a hunch and I asked him what they looked like."

"Who?"

"The man and the boy. I asked him to describe the man and the child."

"And?"

"He said the man wasn't wearing much, but he was a blond in his late twenties. The only thing he could say about the little boy was that he had brown hair and eyes and the man called him Travis. That description matched the child who had died, supposedly accidentally, and an alarm sounded in my head."

"What did you do?"

"After he signed a sworn statement, I let the fuel man leave so he wouldn't get into trouble with his dispatcher. I shook his hand and promised to notify the owners about the verbal abuse, but I knew as I watched him pull his rig out of the parking lot that I had more interesting things to do. The first was to investigate the records, and as soon as I did, I found that a man named Dickens, who fit Mr. Perry's description of the blond man, was the swimming counselor. I got right onto the phone with the owner of the camp, and then, as quickly as I could, got together a group of people who had been near the waterfront at around the time of the accident." He looked at his watch again. "Swanson!"

"They've got it down at the prosecutor's office," the file clerk responded.

"Why?"

"It got pulled when he didn't show up for parole, and then after we started getting reports that he might be that highway murderer, we sent it to the prosecutor."

"What the hell did they need it for? They can't prosecute the low-life until he's caught, can they? Besides, they've got their own copies."

"They can't find theirs."

"Tell them to get their butts over here with my copy now!"

"I tried that, sir. They said that they are short-handed. They said that everyone in the state has been looking for this guy and asked why you're so special that you should have the file."

"Give me that idiot's number. I want to ream him out myself."

"It's a she."

"I don't give a damn. Get her on the phone."

"Let me talk to her," Wright said. "You'll only scare her away."

Hamlon looked at the new guy. Maybe what he said was true. When the phone on his desk rang, he motioned for Wright to handle the call. The way the guy finessed the woman on the other end was phenomenal, positively impressive. "It'll be here in ten minutes," Wright said. "Finish explaining the case to me so I can help out."

"Okay." Hamlon took a sip of his coffee. "By the next day I had sworn testimony that all the people involved had noticed that Dickens was trying to work with Travis, but no one had seen anything else. The accident had happened when most of them were away from the waterfront, on their way back to the bunks to change for lunch. That was where Dickens claimed to be too, at the time the boy went into the deep water off the dock. He also gave sworn testimony, claiming that the boy was fine when he left him at the door to his bunk, well away from the waterfront. The case was at a dead end. I just knew that Dickens was lying. He was an s.o.b. if I ever saw one. Yet there were no witnesses to the actual accident, so there was no case."

"But you said you arrested him. How?"

"I went over the counselor list again, and noticed one name, Darcy Spectrum, that they had omitted from the list of people to be questioned. This Darcy was a young counselor-in-training, and she admitted that she saw Dickens throw the boy into the water and stand there watching while the boy gasped and pleaded. She had tried to get to him, but Dickens threatened her with bodily harm. She said he got into the water himself, and told her not to worry, that he'd pull the boy out. She heard him soothing the boy, telling him he'd hold him up while he kicked and she went back to her bunk.

"When they found the body, she was devastated. She started to speak up but Dickens took her aside and told her again that he would hurt her, and hurt her badly, if she did. She left camp the day after the accident, saying the whole thing was too sad, and the owners understood. After she went home, she made every effort to put the incident out of her mind. That was all I needed. The coroner's report was reviewed in-depth, and Dickens was brought in. But he was one tough nut. He saw himself as Mr. Clean, who never did anything that anyone didn't deserve, according to him. That was the key."

"How so?"

"He blamed everyone else for the trouble he found himself in. It was Darcy's fault for saying those things about him, his wife's fault for saying he had a temper, and most amazingly, Travis's fault for not learning how to swim and acting like such a baby. He outright admitted that he had thrown him into the water on purpose, but claimed it was not his fault that the kid had died."

"So you got a conviction?"

"Yes. And after his sentencing, the camp was sued by the parents of the victim and all the other campers for recklessly endangering their children by employing a maniac. Court documents alleged that the owners, who had employed him for three summers, should have checked his background more thoroughly. They said that his resume should have been considered suspect since he was always available when they needed a swim counselor, yet he was not a teacher, the only profession that ordinarily had summers off to work in camps. Every case that went to a jury was a disaster for the camp owners, and there was no money left for the settlements they had made out of court. They had no choice but to close down and file for bankruptcy. Several people in the area lost their jobs and businesses over the whole thing, including my brother-in-law, and it was not until only two or three years ago that the camp reopened, with new owners and a new name. All this was because of one mean man."

"But why are you looking for him now?"

Hamlon filled him in on the call from New Jersey. "This guy is suspected of five more murders and a kidnapping." He explained what they needed to do. "We'd better get started."

Lori knew she could not stay in the room all day. She would have to come out sooner or later, at least to eat. She was already hungry, but she was scared to death at the thought of having to face him.

After a long, almost eerie silence, she heard him thrashing around in the kitchen. It sounded like he was throwing pots at the walls. The decision was out of her hands. It was time to find some way to get out, or at least somewhere to hide.

She took a good look around. There were two windows in this corner room, one opposite the door and one on the wall next to the first. If she went out either one, she would be on the roof of the front porch.

For a moment she considered where she could go from there. If she could get down to the ground without him seeing her, then she could run away. But although she had looked around carefully on their walk the day before, she did not know where to run. She did not even know where the road out of the camp led. And she was sure that there was nothing around for miles.

The closed bedroom door mocked her at the same time it offered no protection. She had to try to leave. It was time to get ready.

The first thing that she had to do was put on warm clothes. There was no possibility that she could get her coat, because it was downstairs, but she could put several sweaters on over her blouse. She looked in the closet and the dresser drawers and selected what she needed.

She put everything on, ending up with a very large brightly flowered sweater, and she topped it off with a ridiculous knit hat she had found in the dresser. Instead of the new shoes he had bought her, she put on the boots she had been wearing when she was kidnapped, and sat down to think while she laced them up. Maybe it would be better to wait until he went to sleep, but a crash that sounded like a stack of dishes dropping to the floor told her that she did not have time. The next series of noises she heard made her think that he was banging away on something with a heavy object, maybe a frying pan. Her eyes squeezed shut involuntarily with each new strike, and she shuddered over and over, imagining that it was her body being battered.

It seemed clear that he would come for her soon. Now

that he knew the truth, she would undoubtedly be his next victim. Then he would probably wait a while and go back for Jackie. Then Jackie would have to go through all of this. Even though he was Jackie's father, Lori was sure she would hate it.

She decided it was time to act when she heard the next round of noise. This time it was the tinkling of breaking glass, followed by thumping. That was when she pushed the dresser across the wooden planks of the floor and in front of the door.

Suddenly the banging stopped. She moved into action at the same time she heard him start up the stairs.

Opening a window as quietly as she could, she stepped out onto the pitched roof of the porch. Almost immediately, he started knocking on her door.

"Go away," she called, trying to keep her voice even, and still project it over the pounding on the door. She reached in to close the curtains and cut down on the cold air that she supposed was rushing into the room. "I'm not talking to you, Daddy."

He stopped knocking, and seemed to be thinking. Then his voice erupted through the door, and he resumed pounding on it. "No! You're not my little girl. She has a beauty mark on her stomach and you don't have it."

"It wasn't beautiful," she said, from the ledge. "I hated it and had it removed. Didn't you ever hear of laser surgery?"

He seemed to consider that. For a while it was very quiet. "Maybe I was wrong, sweetheart," he said, in a much softer tone. "Can we talk about it?"

She barely heard what he was saying as she slid down the roof.

"Please, honey, won't you open the door? I admitted I was wrong. Now I'm gonna have this whole big mess to clean up, just because I didn't stop to think."

She let go of the gutter and dropped to the ground. She

could not hear what he was saying anymore, but she hoped he would keep talking, until she could find a place to hide.

Which way to go? She headed for the road, keeping as close to the buildings as she could, until she was out of sight of the house.

Lori knew he would be after her as soon as he discovered she was missing. It was important for her to find a place to hide until dark. But where? He knew every building, as he had shown when they took their walk. Surely there was no place in any of them to hide.

She wondered if he had left the keys in the car, and if she could get it started before he could catch up with her. But it was parked in front of the house, and she could not risk going back there.

Maybe she should go to the boathouse and row across the lake to the other side. She had tried to see if there were houses on the other shore when they were out yesterday, but didn't spot any, although she couldn't be sure. Should she take the chance and try? What if he got another boat and followed her? Or what if he shot at her before she could get away?

She crouched down in the shadow of the recreation hall. What should she do?

They were the longest hours Wally had ever been through. She kept worrying that even if the police got there, and found that was where Dickens had brought Lori, she may have convinced him that she was not Jackie, and he may have done something to her. But her biggest fear was that they would not be there at all and there would be no more leads. Or worse, that no one would take her seriously and they would not even try to find Lori there.

Finally Elliot called back. "They are going to check. I just got a call, and they think we're onto something."

Wally grasped the edge of her table, as relief mixed with her other fears flooded over her. "Please keep me posted."

* * *

Jackie had not answered him in almost five minutes. This was ridiculous. He was the father, not her. He banged on the door again. "Jackie, for the last time, let me in."

No answer.

Dickens shivered. It felt a little cold in the house. Suspicious, he reached down and felt the floor. There was a breeze coming from under her door.

Why would she have the window open in this weather? He banged on the door. "You'll catch your death of cold," he said. He had forgotten to buy a blow dryer, and he still felt guilty about that. "Your hair is wet!"

There was still no answer, and it was getting colder and colder in the hall. He had to get in there.

He pushed as hard as he could against the door. It made him angrier when he realized that she had blocked the door, and suddenly an awareness hit him, clearing the doubts and confirming his suspicions that this girl was not his daughter. Finally, he felt whatever was in front of the door slide a little. He pushed harder, and steadily, and finally got the door open enough to see inside. The window was wide open and the room was empty.

He roared with rage on his way down the stairs and bolted out the front door.

Chapter Twenty-three

Hamlon took his eyes off the road only long enough to glance with irritation at the clock on his dashboard, then went right back to watching the blacktop disappear rapidly beneath his police cruiser. On either side of his car, the landscape seemed to speed by, bleak and brown under the gray November sky. The radio on his dashboard crackled with life, murmuring coded instructions in case their quarry had a police scanner of his own. As the three patrol cars led by Hamlon sped toward the camp, two more were coming from the other direction. But they were not covering the nearly thirty miles quickly enough.

There was no longer any doubt in Hamlon's mind that Dickens was up at that camp. While he was waiting for the other troopers to arrive at the station, he and Wright made some calls and got substantiation for his gut feeling that Levine was right. He had several positive sightings, including one from an all-night gas station right off the highway. It was less than fifty miles away and helped to pinpoint the time that they had arrived at the campsite as two days earlier.

Hamlon's foot itched to floor the gas pedal, but he had to maintain his pace. Time was a real factor. They were set to sneak in under the cover of approaching darkness and would be able to start moving into position at about 4:30. He could barely wait. He wanted to catch this guy so badly he could practically taste it.

All of the planning for the raid had taken time, but it was finally done, and they were moving. Hamlon settled down in his seat for the last few miles of highway before the turnoff onto the secondary road.

Lori could hear him racing past the recreation hall. She was inside, behind the stage, under the folds of an old musty curtain, and hoped that he would think she had kept running and gone down the road. It would give her time to figure out what to do. She did not move, and barely breathed. If only her heart didn't have to beat so loudly.

A few minutes later he ran back the other way, his footfalls making dull thuds on the muddy ground, and seconds after that she heard the car. He was going after her with it, and would find out soon that she hadn't left the campground, because he would not catch up with her along the road.

She couldn't stay where she was. She knew, even as she was making them, that her footprints would show in the dust on the floor. Wherever she hid, they would lead right to her.

Lori had to think.

He came driving back up the road, slowly, like he was looking for her everywhere. From her position in the rafters of the boat house, Lori could see out of the window, even though it was streaked with dirt, and she watched as he drove from building to building and checked each one. He was moving closer and closer to the lake.

She hoped her plan would work. She'd had to come up

with it quickly. But since putting it into irreversible action and climbing out of the way, or so she hoped, she had thought of at least seven ways she could have done it better.

There was no way to go back and fix it. For now she had to live with what she had done, and pray that it would work until she could outmaneuver him. She looked at her watch and then at the position of the sun. With any luck, the setting sun would cooperate.

He got out of the car at the top of the rocky path that wound down to the lake. He moved down it quickly, slipping and sliding on the loose pebbles, and stopped at the door to the boathouse. Lori heard his hand on the latch, and the sharp click as he pushed against the metal. Then he released it suddenly, and she watched through a knothole in the floor of the loft as he turned and gazed out over the lake.

She knew what he was seeing, but hoped that he would not see it exactly that way. With any luck, he would think there was a person, hopefully her, in the boat, rowing away from the dock.

Lori shivered. Not only were her feet soaked from pushing the boat as far and as hard as she could out into the lake, but she had taken off her top sweater. It was the brightly flowered one, and she put it and the stupid hat on the huge coil of rope that she found on the dock. It had been unbelievably heavy, and she could barely manage to slide it into the boat, which she had to take out of the boathouse and drag to the lake.

It was okay that she left a trail. That was what she wanted: to have all the signs point to the lake. She had to walk, still in the lake, around to the other side of the boathouse to get out, so that she would not leave footprints on her way back in. The smell of the waterlogged wood as she crawled inside had made her want to sneeze, but she somehow held it back.

The latch snapped open again, and before Lori could take

a deep breath to hold, he came in. She froze up, and prayed. *Don't look up, don't look up, don't look up.* He took another row boat, and a pair of oars, and pulled them out and down to the lake.

Go after the boat, go after the boat, go after the boat.

The handheld radios were in frequent use between the officers involved in the chase. "Make sure to avoid hitting the girl, but watch out for Dickens. He is armed and extremely dangerous." The reminder felt painful coming from Hamlon's lips, clenched as they were. He stomped his feet to remove some of the tension.

"Check on the positions," he said a few minutes later. The other cars had finally come from the farther side of the county, and one of them took up a place at the edge of the road that led into the camp. The other moved further in, and prepared to cover the far side of the lake. Hamlon received a curt affirmative from both of them.

It was time to move up into the campsite.

That brat had a head start, and if she could get across the damned lake and out of the water onto the path that led to the road, she would find that old couple who lived there year 'round. They might try to help her, but he would take care of all of them. Karl was really angry now. This wasn't his fault, it was hers, and Jackie's mother's. If that were even Jackie. She wasn't, he had decided for sure. Right? He was so mixed up that his head hurt. That was their fault too. Well, he would make them pay. He would make them all pay.

Lori counted to five hundred in her head. Then she looked out to see how far he had gotten. She knew that any minute he would realize that there was no one in the boat. The oars were just drifting, not really moving at all. She dreaded what would happen if they made the boat go in a circle.

So far he was going after it, but he was rowing strongly and gaining every second. She quickly climbed down and ran out of the boathouse to the car.

Please have left the keys, please have left the keys, please have . . . She pulled the door open and jumped into the driver's seat. The keys were in the ignition.

Don't flood the engine, don't flood the engine, don't flood the engine.

The car started, and she backed it up. Her driving skills were still rather new, but she did not take as much care as she had been taught. She turned the car around and headed down the road as fast as she could go.

The light was fading as she left the campgrounds. She could see that the road traveled alongside the lake. She kept catching glimpses of it through the trees. It seemed lighter on the lake than on the tree-covered road. There had to be a turnoff somewhere, *please, please,* or she would end up simply going around the whole lake, and be back at the entrance to the camp.

But she did not see any turnoff. She kept going as fast as she could go and still keep the car on the road. Every foot that she put behind her was a foot away from him, and she plunged ahead on the rutted dirt road.

It was particularly dark in one section, because the trees were thick and covered the road. Suddenly the car's automatic headlights came on, and, to her horror, she saw, illuminated in their beams, Jackie's father, standing in the middle of the road. He had the face of a madman, a nightmare.

Lori thought she saw someone running in the woods off to the right but realized it was only her mind playing tricks on her. She was as good as dead, and she knew it. He would get her now. Unless she got him.

Gripping the wheel tightly, Lori knew there was no way

to stop the man, unless she stopped him first. She aimed
the car straight at him.

A look of terror came over his face that almost matched
the way Lori felt. He jumped to the side, but she turned
the steering wheel, determined to finally get him. She
waited for the horrible thud she knew she would hear.

But instead she heard scraping and felt the car sliding
sideways as it slid off the road into a ditch. She could not
move it. Her tires spun even when she tried frantically to
go into reverse.

He yanked open her door, with his gun pointed straight
at her. She squeezed her eyes shut and put her hands over
her head.

"Goodbye, witch," he said.

"Don't move," a voice said, but it wasn't his. This one
was deeper and even more menacing. "Drop the gun."

It seemed to take forever before the cold pressure of the
gun was off Lori's temple, but finally it was gone. That
was when she realized that she was not breathing. She let
out her breath, and dared to open her eyes. A giant of a
policeman was standing there and he actually had a smile
on his face.

"It's okay, Lori," he said softly. "I'm here to take you
home. It's all over. You're safe now." She could not believe she was looking at a police officer and that he knew
her name.

She watched as Jackie's father was read his rights and
placed into a police car. The policeman reached his hand
out to help her out of the driver's seat of the car. Then he
held her as she sobbed into his shoulder.

When she had finished, he wrapped her in a blanket and
helped her into his car. Reaching for the radio, he said, "I
think there may be some people who want to hear from
you."

* * *

Elliot called right after the dinner that nobody ate. "They got her and she's okay," he said, in a rush of words.

Wally felt as if her heart would burst. She motioned to Nate and Debbie that things were okay. They each gave her two thumbs up back. "How?"

"It was really close. The team got there just as he was about to shoot her."

A sickening chill ran up Wally's spine. "At the campsite?"

"On the road leading to it. She had actually escaped, but he rowed across the lake to catch up with her. The road apparently led around it."

"Oh!"

"You were right about where to find her," Elliot said, with approval in his voice. "How did you know?"

"I'll explain later," Wally said, as waves of relief washed the tension out of her. "Did you tell her parents?"

"Yes," Elliot said. He chuckled. "I have to admit that you weren't the first one we called. The police up in Minnesota went to the camp as soon as we tipped them off. I had a devil of a time convincing them to even go look there, since I didn't know why you suggested it, but I found one officer who agreed. He and his team found them right outside."

"When will she be home?" Wally asked.

"She's being flown in tomorrow morning. Dickens is behind bars again, on more charges than he can count."

"Had he figured out that she wasn't Jackie?"

"I don't have those details. Now will you tell me how you knew?"

"How about if you come over after you've done your paperwork? I'll bet you haven't had dinner, and I have plenty. I'll keep it warm for you." Then she added, "We're all waiting to hear about this."

He was quiet for a minute. Wally supposed he was

weighing the invitation in his mind, and might even be wondering who "all" was.

"Okay," he said finally. "I'll be there as soon as I can."

Elliot's elation enabled him to do the paperwork in record time, even with all the congratulatory interruptions he and Dominique received, but he had to fight his way through a barrage of reporters who wanted to get his version of the story. "No comment," he said, "except to say that we are all happy that she was found safely."

He drove over to the Morris's bursting with the story. He had only been able to get a few more details since he called her, but he could not wait to tell Mr. and Mrs. Morris about them, and Debbie, too, he hoped.

Before going to bed, Wally did not spare Nate a complete recital of all she had done to help find Lori. After she proudly spelled out the particulars for the sixth or seventh time, he had finally given in and admitted that what she did was admirable. Added to that, she pointed out, was the obvious fact that their daughter was smitten by a wonderful, intelligent young man, and vice versa. While Nate would not give her credit for that, he agreed she was probably correct.

Chapter Twenty-four

Wally knew that Debbie had been up late with Elliot, based on what time she had finally heard the front door close, and she tiptoed around the house, even while she thought her feet could barely be touching the floor. Since she had awakened she had been unable to do anything but run around the house, finish cleaning the kitchen after their triumphant dinner the night before, and finally, when she got into the steamy shower, sing loudly with joy. Afterwards, she made Nate and Debbie a big breakfast, and took Sammy for a nice long walk. Wally had a lot of things to do. Thanksgiving was the next day and she was not nearly ready. And there was one more loose end. There might be another guest. She hoped that Elliot would accept her invitation, extended at dinner the night before. He'd said he'd have to see if his aunt would understand why he was canceling.

Now all she needed was a parking space near the grocery store.

He paced around his cell. The steel bars and cement cinder blocks were all too familiar. He sat on the cot and cradled his head in his hands. This time he knew that he was never, ever getting out. It was all her fault. That girl had tricked him. He had thought she was his little Jackie, and she let him believe that and she fooled him. After all he had done for her, or anyway for Jackie. It was so confusing. But they shouldn't hold him responsible. Since he had done it for Jackie, killed those people and kidnapped the girl, and since she was not Jackie, someone else should pay. He was always paying for other people's mistakes. And they called it justice.

Here he had made plans to take Jackie to see his relatives in the spring. They would have been so happy to see her that they would let him back into the family. But then this stupid mistake happened. Now they would never love him.

The edge of his metal bunk bed cut into his hand as he gripped it. Jackie's mother was at fault too. She had stolen Jackie away and made him sign away his rights, and he was gonna get her. That was a promise. If he ever got out of jail. Four walls, full of cinder blocks and bars, were his future. He did not deserve this. He was too smart for this.

The guard came in and told him he had a visitor. All the way to the meeting room, he wondered who had come to see him. Maybe it was a reporter, and he could tell his story. No, he thought, he was not going to tell it, unless he got paid. He would hold out for cash. Big money. He might not be able to spend it, but he could get to be a rich man.

He was terribly disappointed when he saw who had come to visit.

"How are you, Karl?" said Lester Crabtree, the public defender who had represented him so many years ago. He was older now, not quite as scrawny. In fact, he had a big round belly. His shirt tails under his cheap suit were still untucked. And his nose looked like he had seen a lot more bourbons since the last time Karl saw him. "Looks like you're in a bit of trouble again."

* * *

Wally was up to her elbows in pie crust for her three pies, pumpkin, apple-cranberry, and lemon meringue, when she turned off the noon news with a self-satisfied push of the remote control button. The footage of the Kaufmans at the airport greeting each other after their ordeal had been extensive, with coverage on all the major channels. As she rolled each crust out, though, she doubted that there would be "more at five and eleven," even though it had been promised. The Kaufmans weren't the type to give interviews.

They really hadn't needed to thank her as much as they did, nor did the mayor, or the high school principal, or the Rabbi.

They were all most welcome, Wally thought, as she wiped her hands to answer the constantly ringing phone again.

"Hello?"

"Mrs. Morris? This is Elliot. About your invitation. I'd love to come for Thanksgiving."

Wally smiled, satisfied. Another loose end was neatly tied up. "Perfect," she replied.